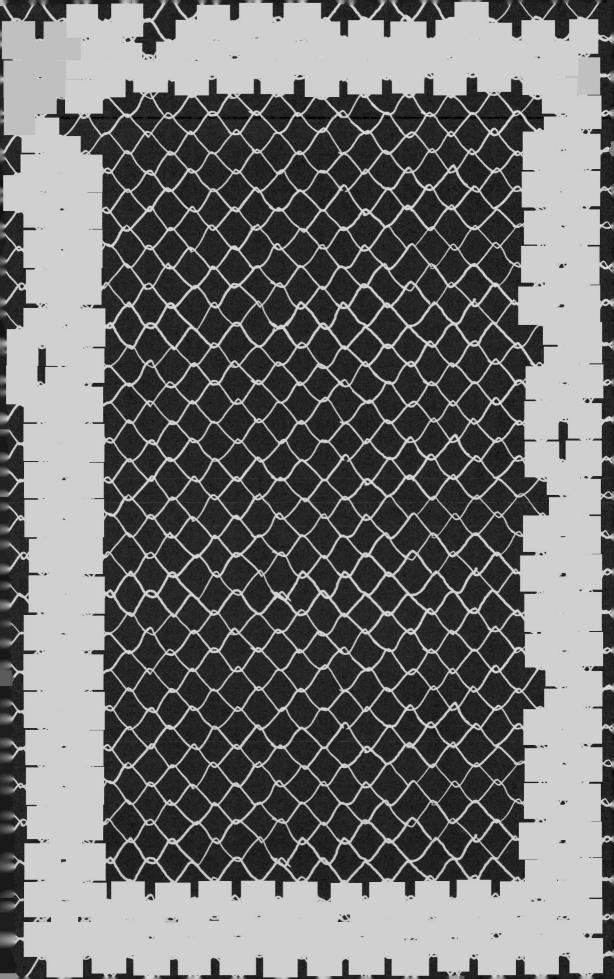

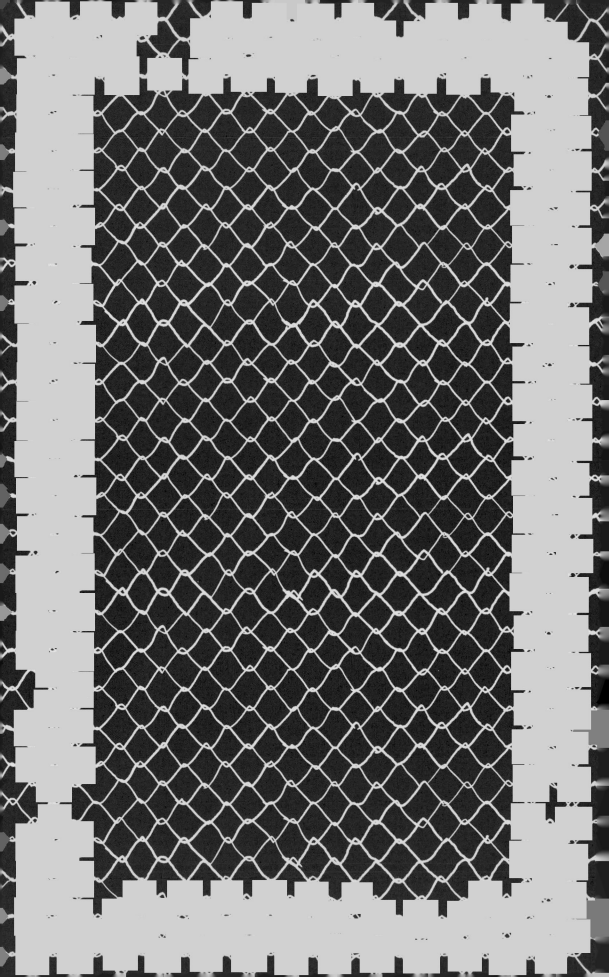

Dirge

We do lie beneath the grass
  In the moonlight, in the shade
  Of the yew-tree. They that pass
  Hear us not. We are afraid
  They would envy our delight,
  In our graves by glow-worm night.
Come follow us, and smile as we;
  We sail to the rock in the ancient waves,
Where the snow falls by thousands into the sea,
  And the drown'd and the shipwreck'd have happy graves.

Thomas Lovell Beddoes (1851)

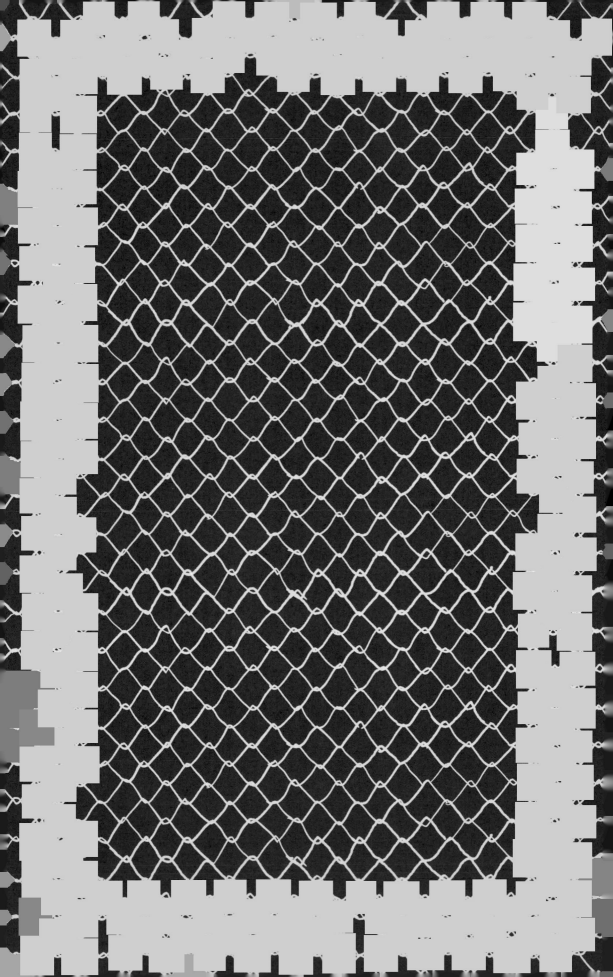

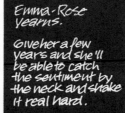

Emma-Rose
yearns.

Give her a few
years and she'll
be able to catch
the sentiment by
the neck and shake
it real hard.

But for now—

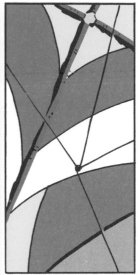

—Emma-Rose,
ten years old,
honey and dirt,
four-foot-four
straight-to-the-
floor, can only
recognize the
feeling her blood
makes as it
rushes past the
place inside
where her future
belongs.

She feels
tomorrow pull.

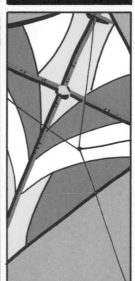

Even back then,
Em wanted.

Em needed.

Em knew then
that, no, this is not
enough.

Imminent, eminent
Emma-Rose,
capital-M for right-
in-the-middle; not
A, not Z. Lucky 13,
the point of no
return, M-the-
meridian between
then and next.

Her name, her
letter, her place:

On a precipice.

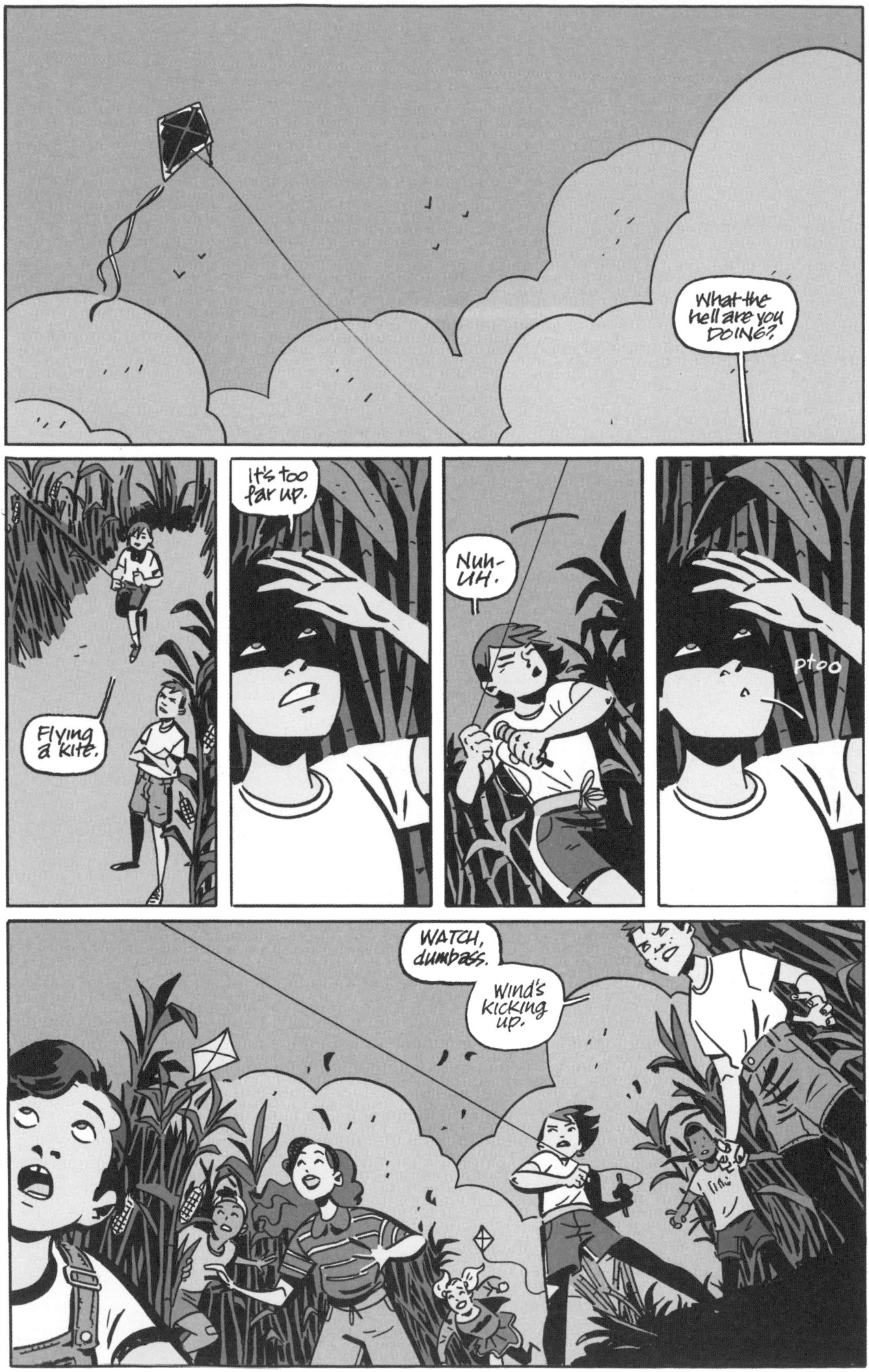

What the hell are you DOING?
Flying a kite.
It's too far up.
Nuh-UH.
ptoo
WATCH, dumbass.
Wind's kicking up.

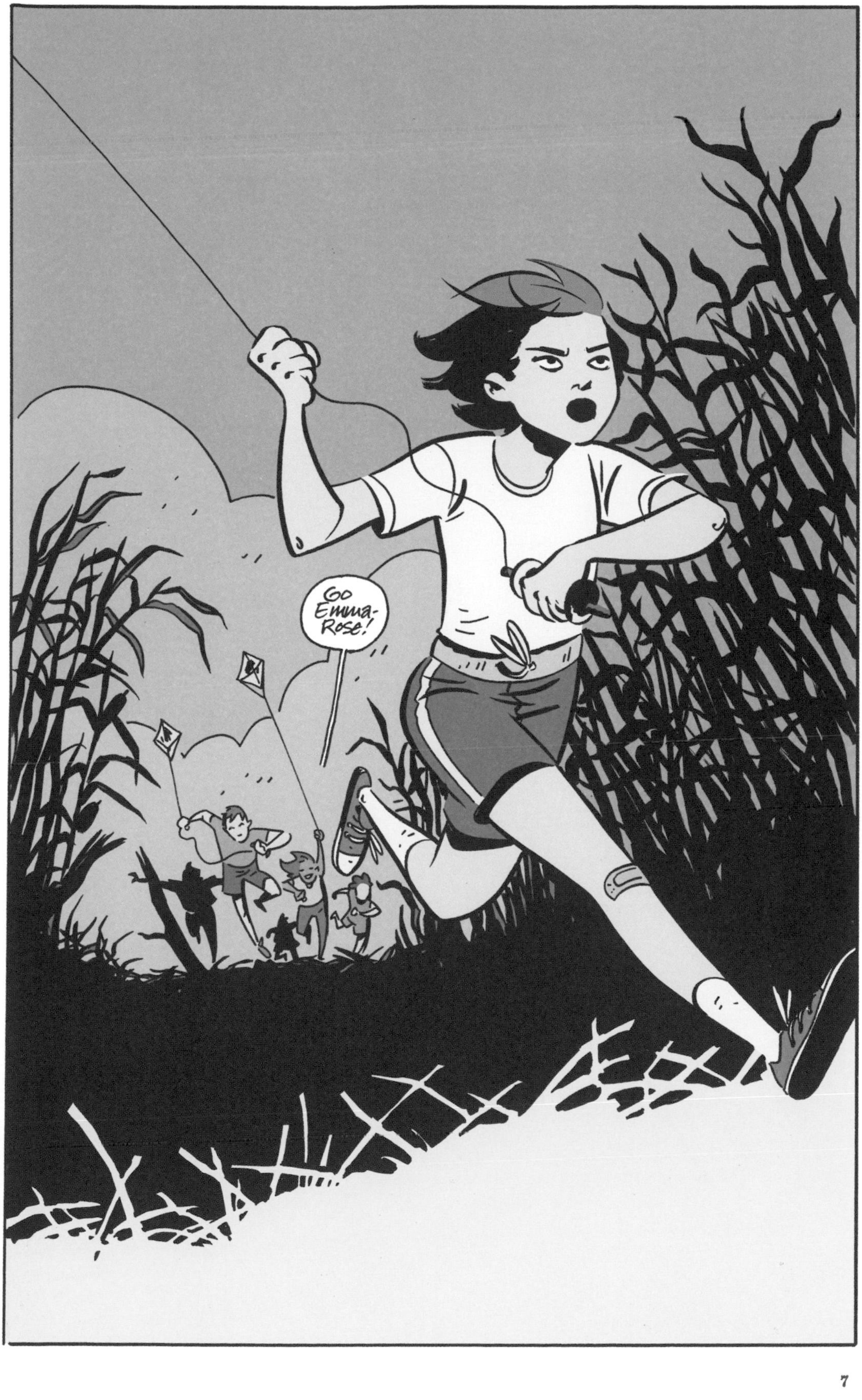
Go Emma-Rose!

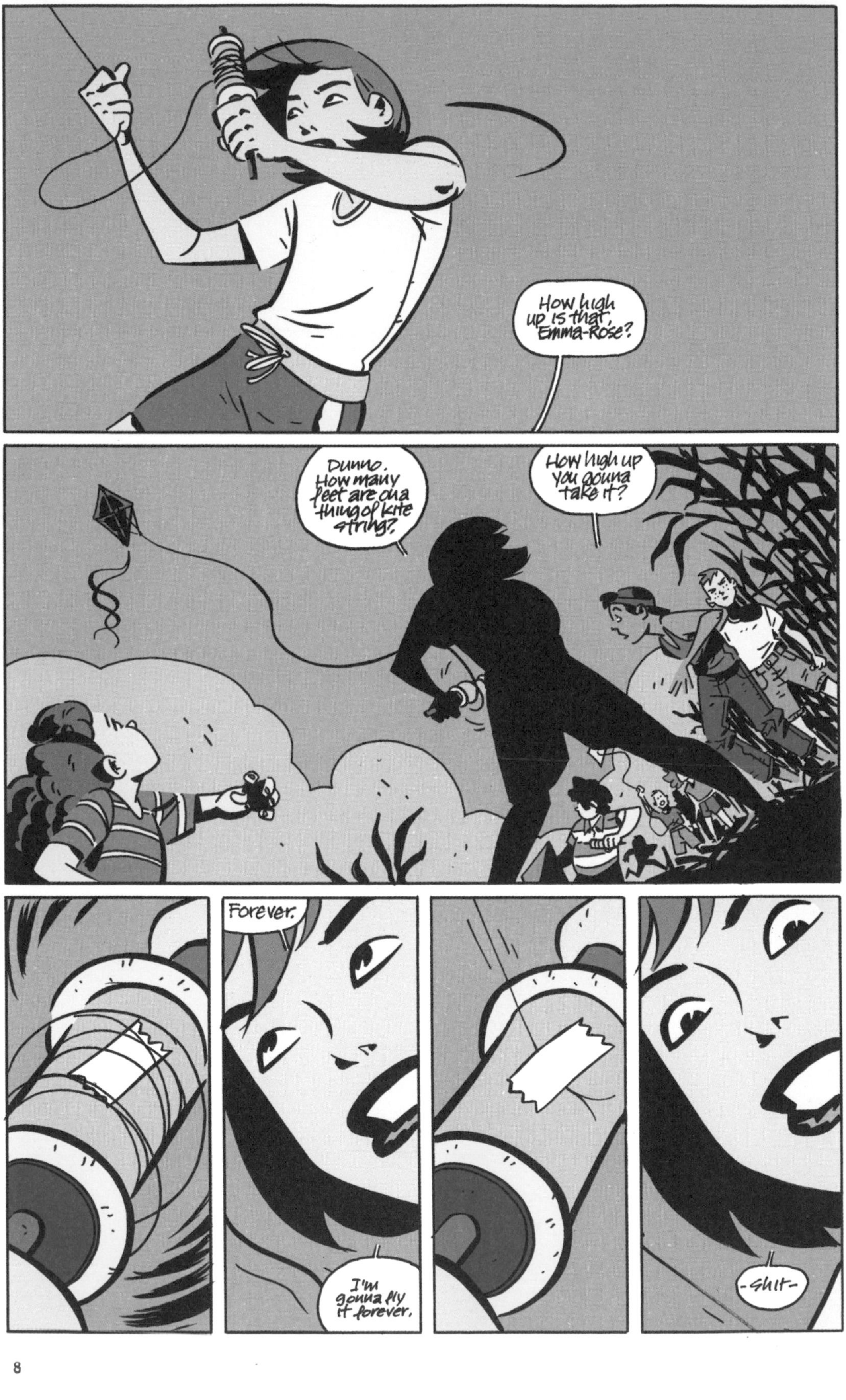

How high up is that, Emma-Rose?
Dunno. How many feet are on a thing of kite string?
How high up you gonna take it?
Forever.
I'm gonna fly it forever.
-Shit-

What a dumbass! She-
can't
ev-
hup
gotcha.
Gimme your string!
Hurry!

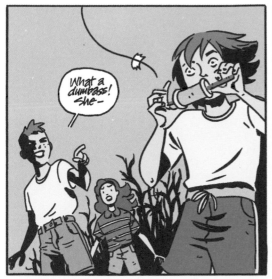

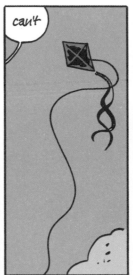

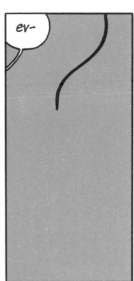

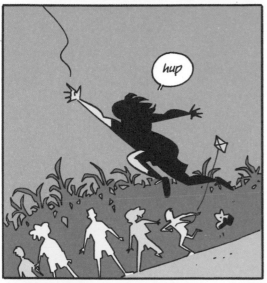

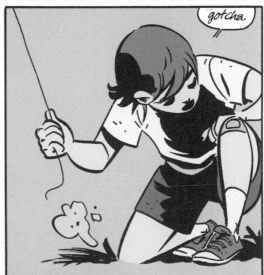

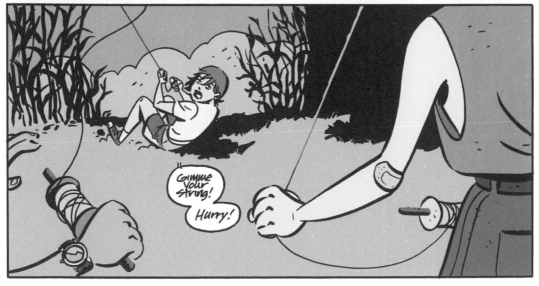

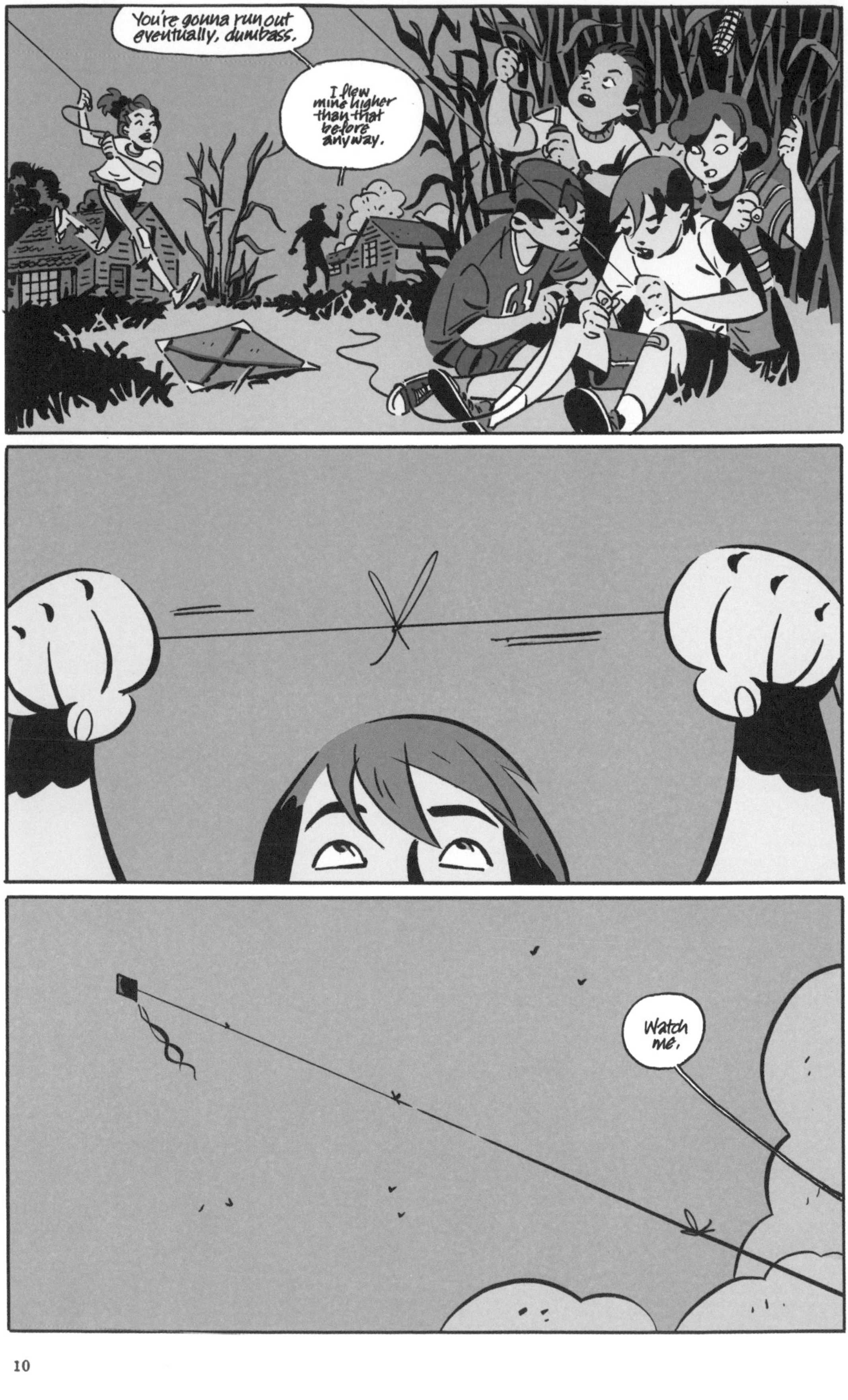
You're gonna run out eventually, dumbass.
I flew mine higher than that before anyway.
Watch me.

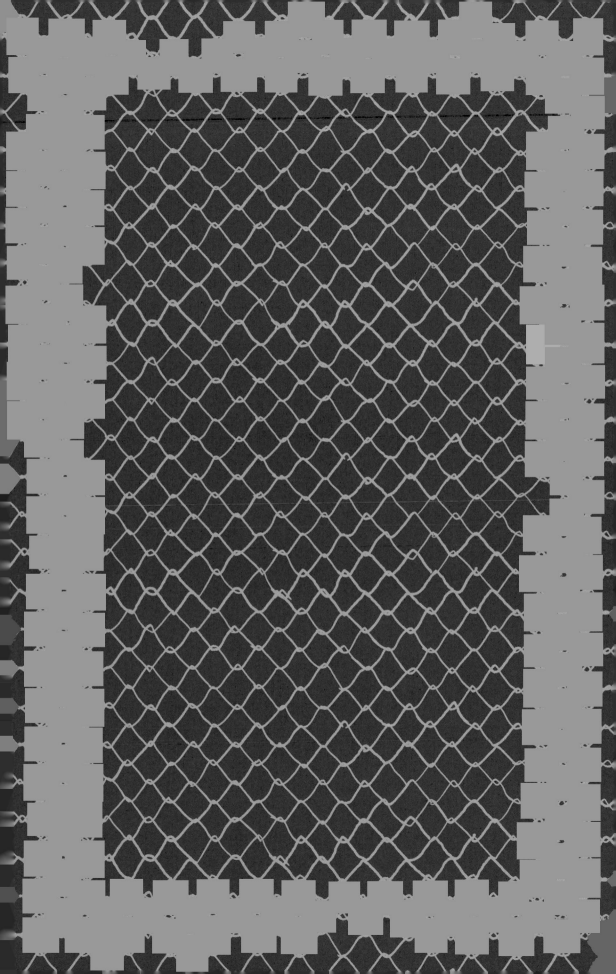

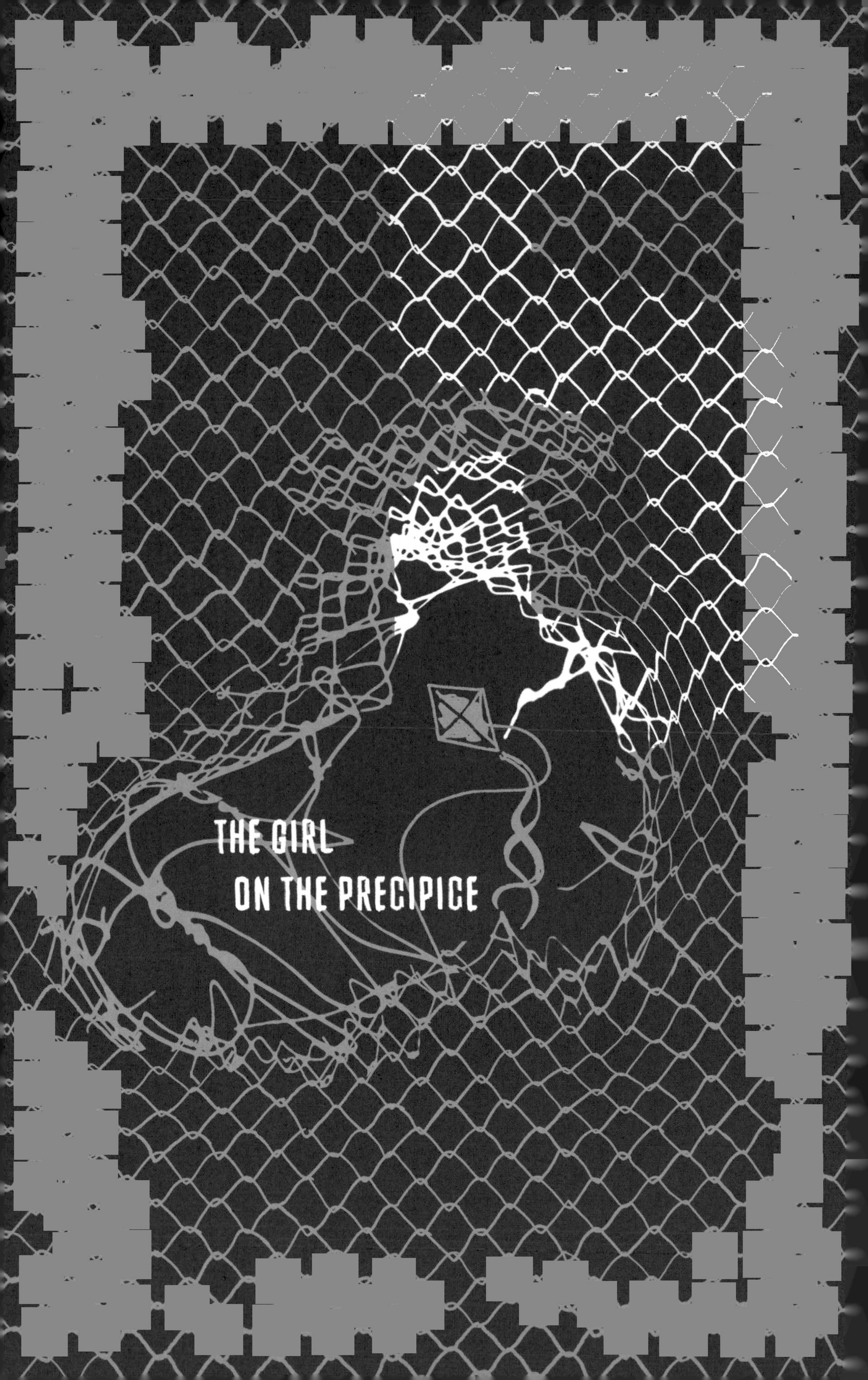
THE GIRL
ON THE PRECIPICE

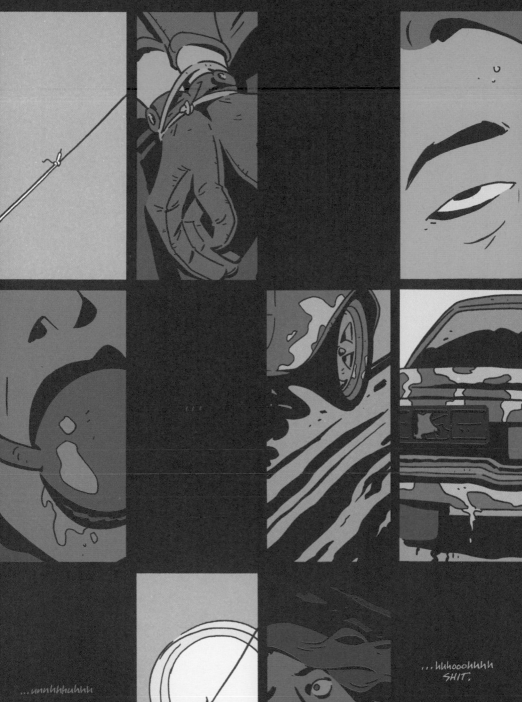

...unnhhhuhhh

...hhhooohhhh
SHIT.

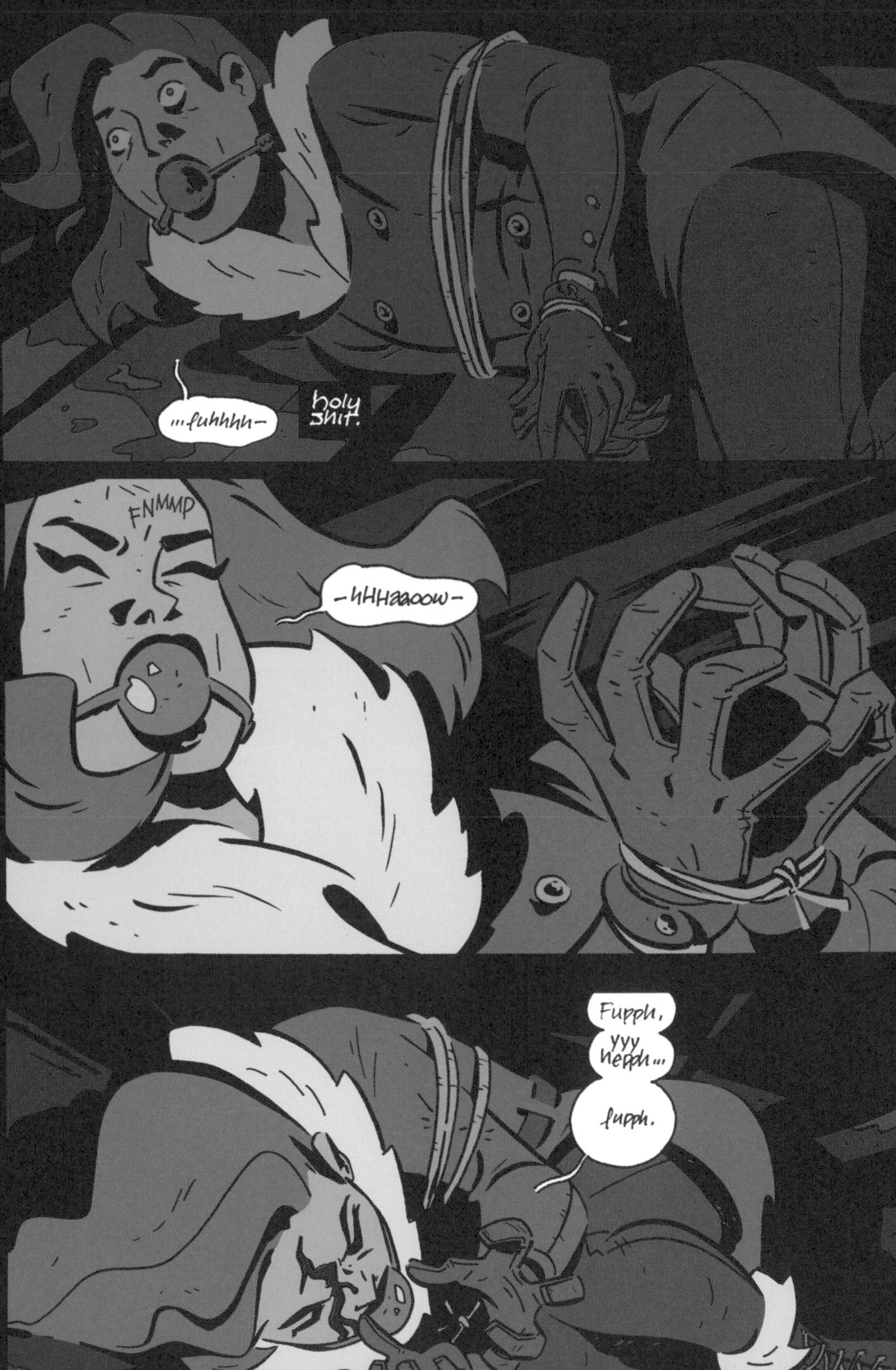
...fuhhhh–
holy shit.
FNMMP
–HHHaaoow–
Fupph, yyy hepph...
fupph.

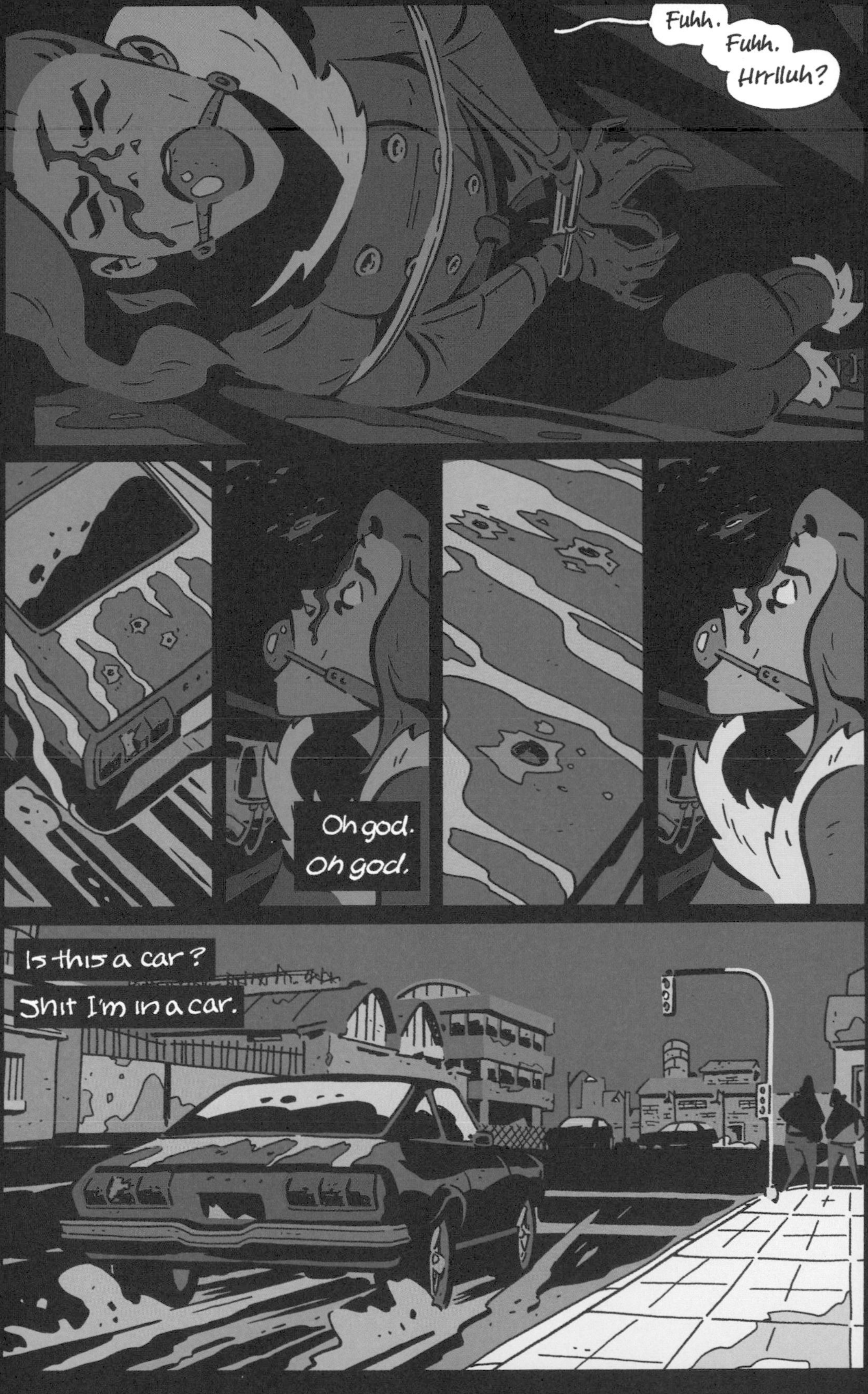
Fuhh.
Fuhh.
Hrrlluh?
Oh god.
Oh god.
Is this a car?
Shit I'm in a car.

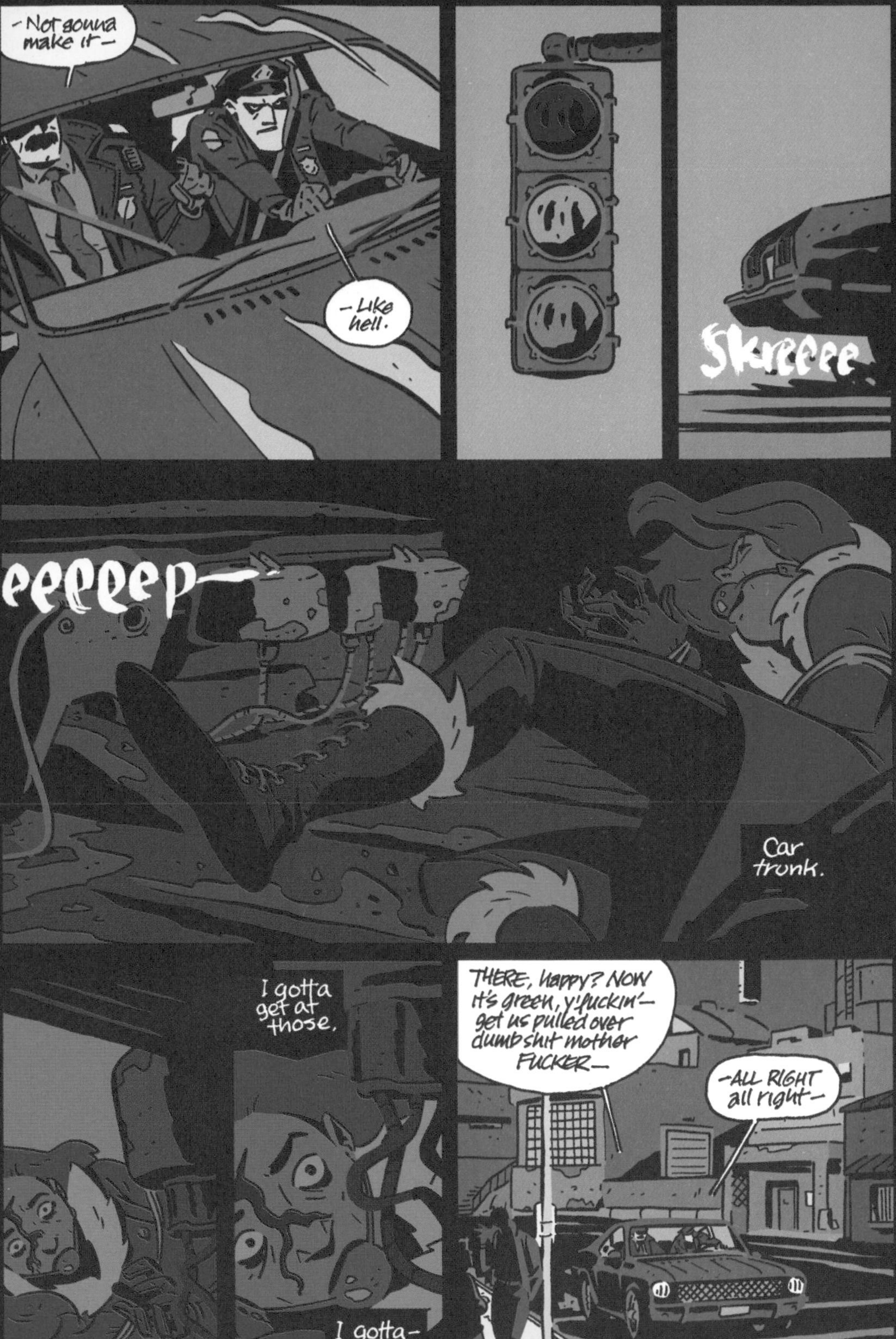
-Not gonna make it-
-Like hell.
Skreeee
eeeep-
Car trunk.
I gotta get at those,
I gotta-
THERE, happy? NOW it's green, y'fuckin'- get us pulled over dumbshit mother FUCKER-
-ALL RIGHT all right-

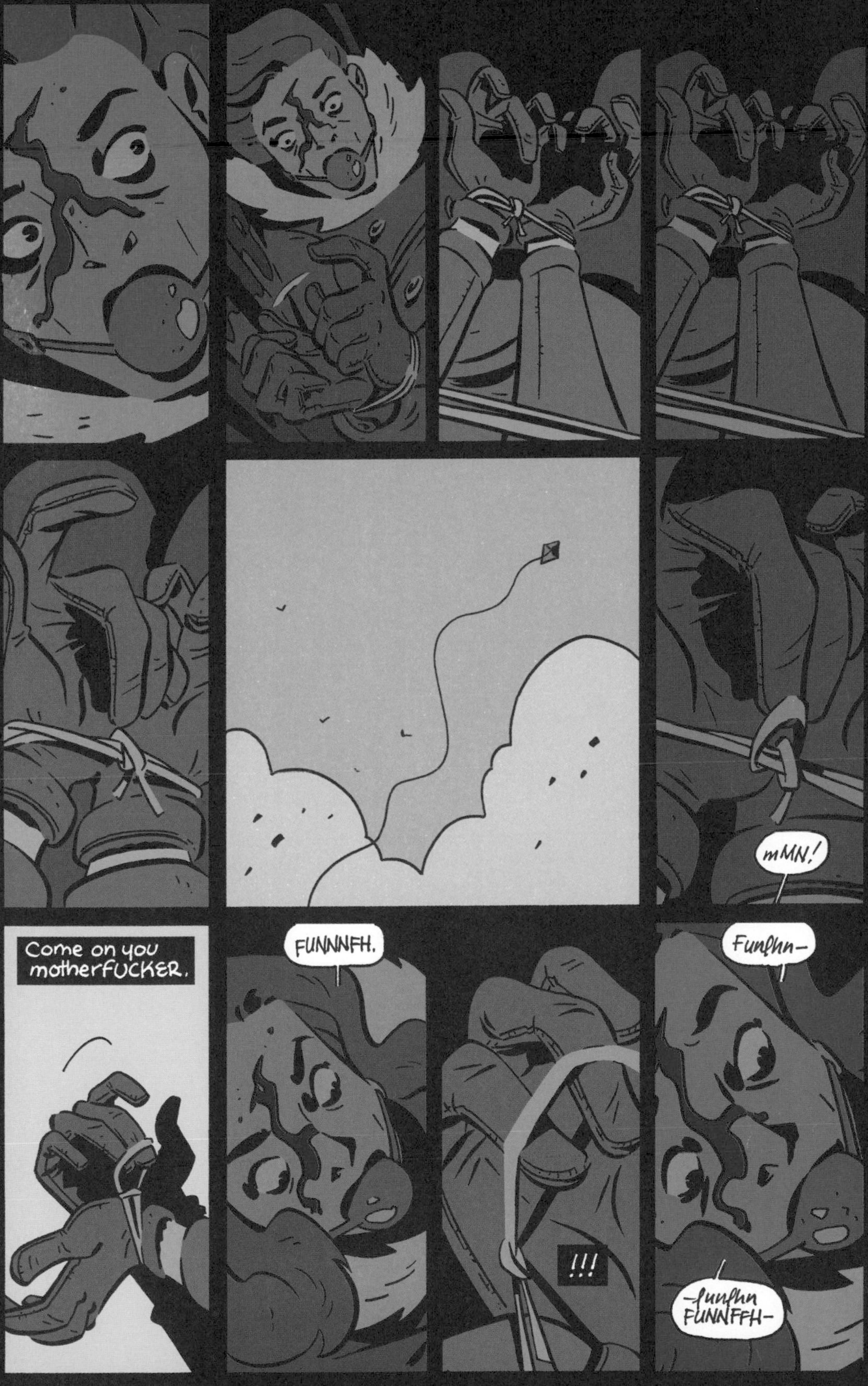
mMN!
Come on you motherFUCKER.
FUNNNFH.
!!!
Funfhn-
-funfhn FUNNFFH-

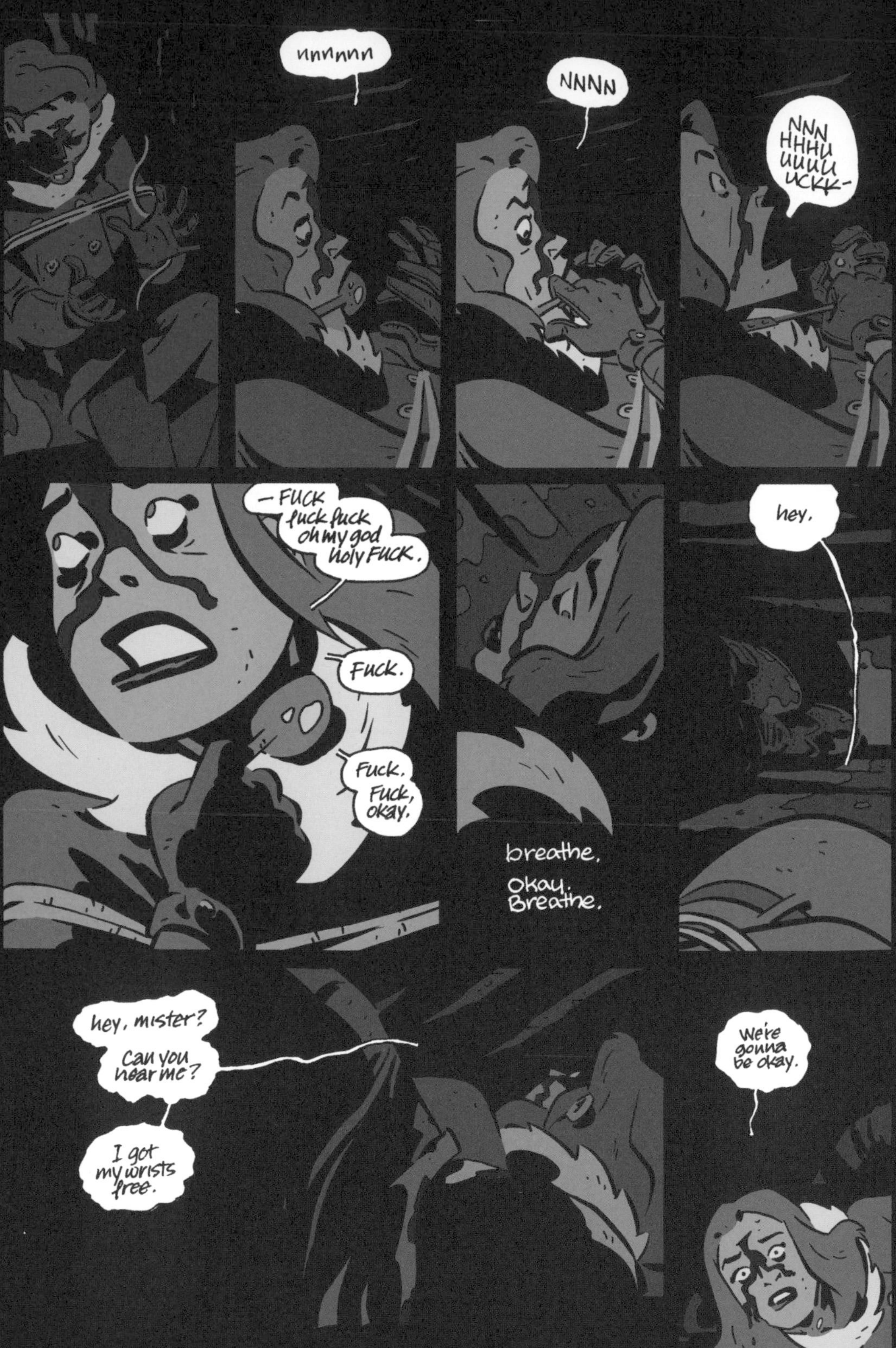
nnnnnn
NNNN
NNN HHHU UUUU UCKK-
—FUCK fuck fuck oh my god holy FUCK.
Fuck.
Fuck. Fuck, okay.
breathe.
Okay. Breathe.
hey.
hey, mister?
Can you hear me?
I got my wrists free.
We're gonna be okay.

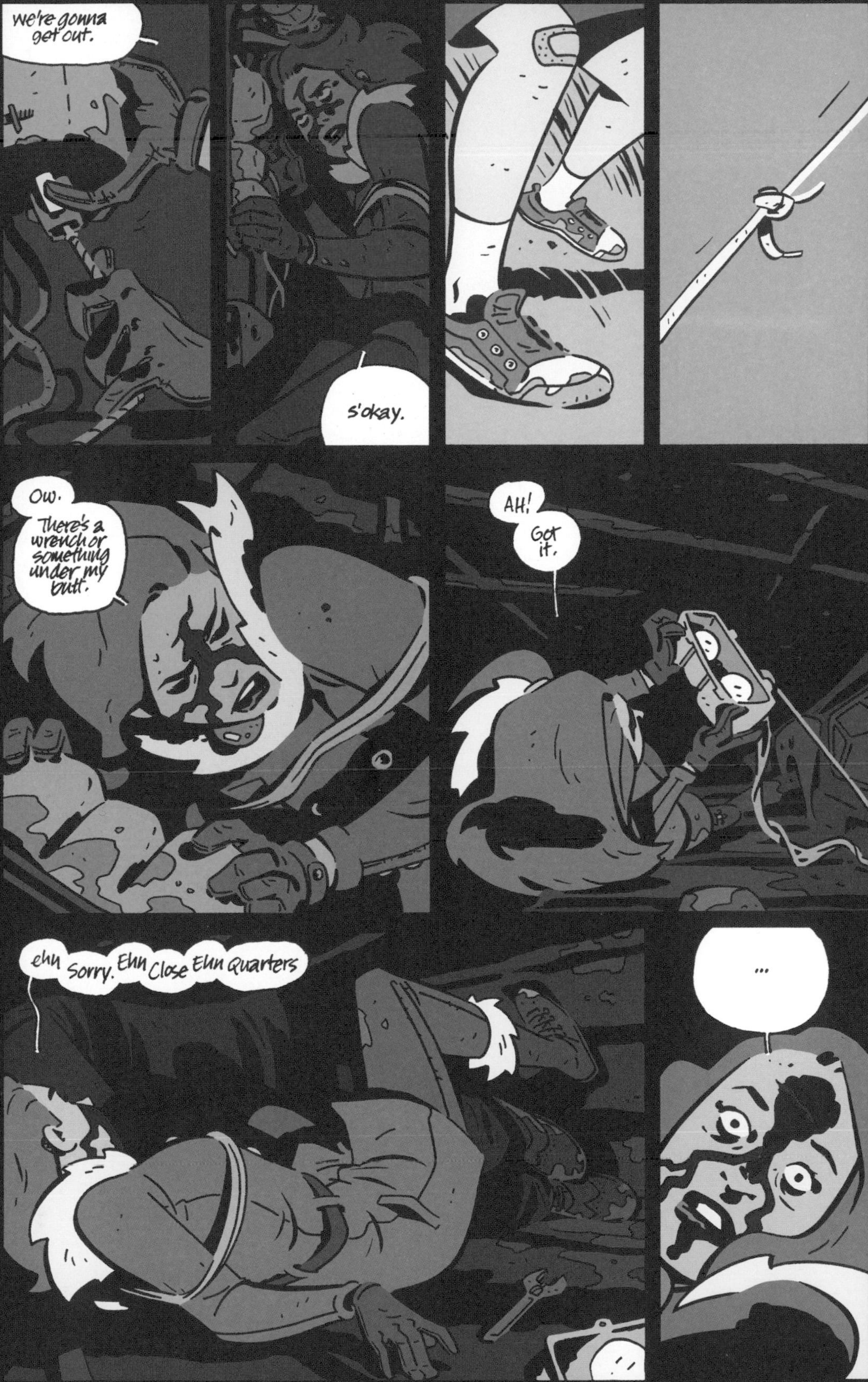
We're gonna get out.
s'okay.
Ow.
There's a wrench or something under my butt.
AH!
Got it.
ehn Sorry. Ehn Close Ehn Quarters
...

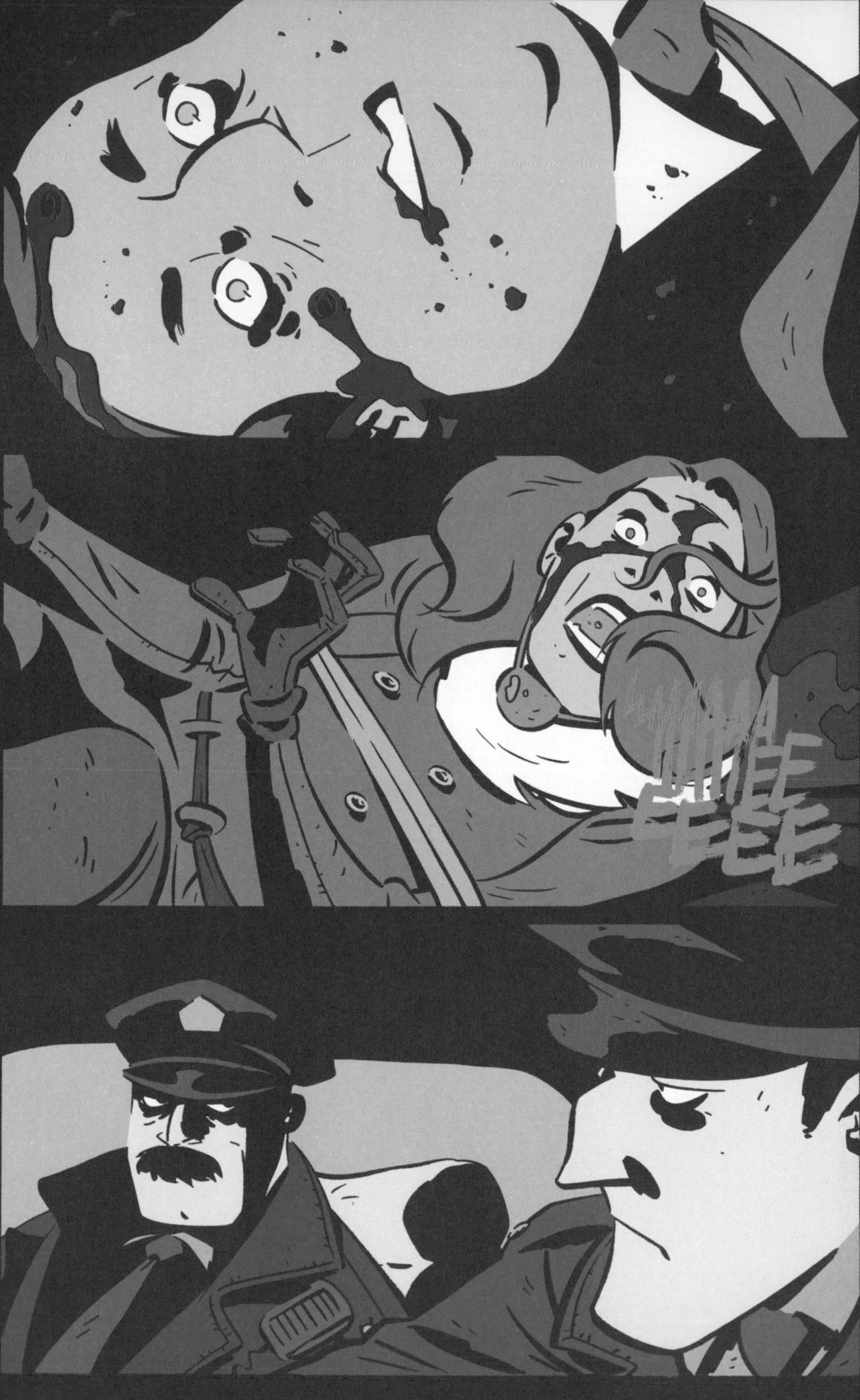

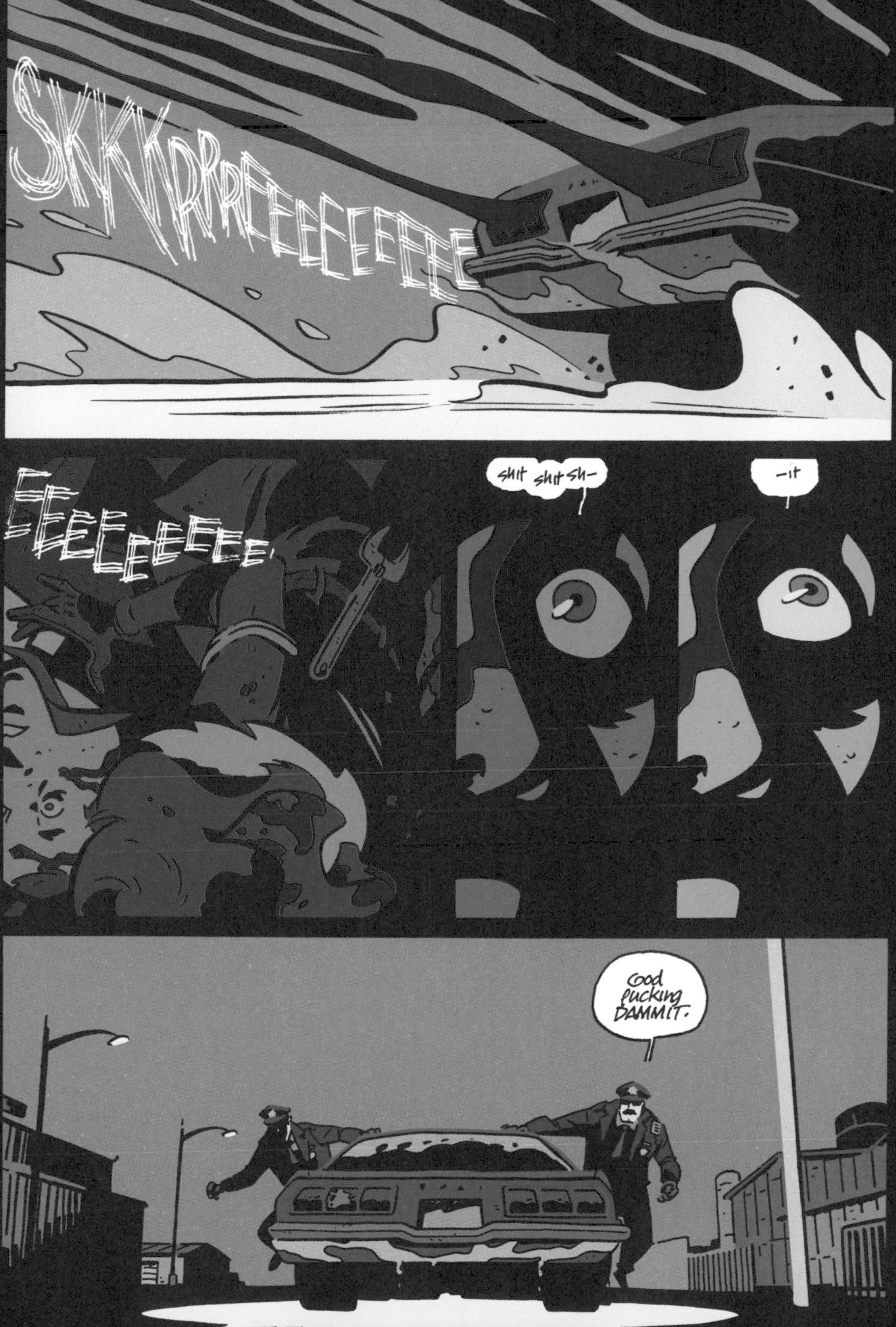
SKKKRRRREEEEEEEEE
EEEEEEEEEEEEE
shit shit sh-
-it
God fucking DAMMIT.

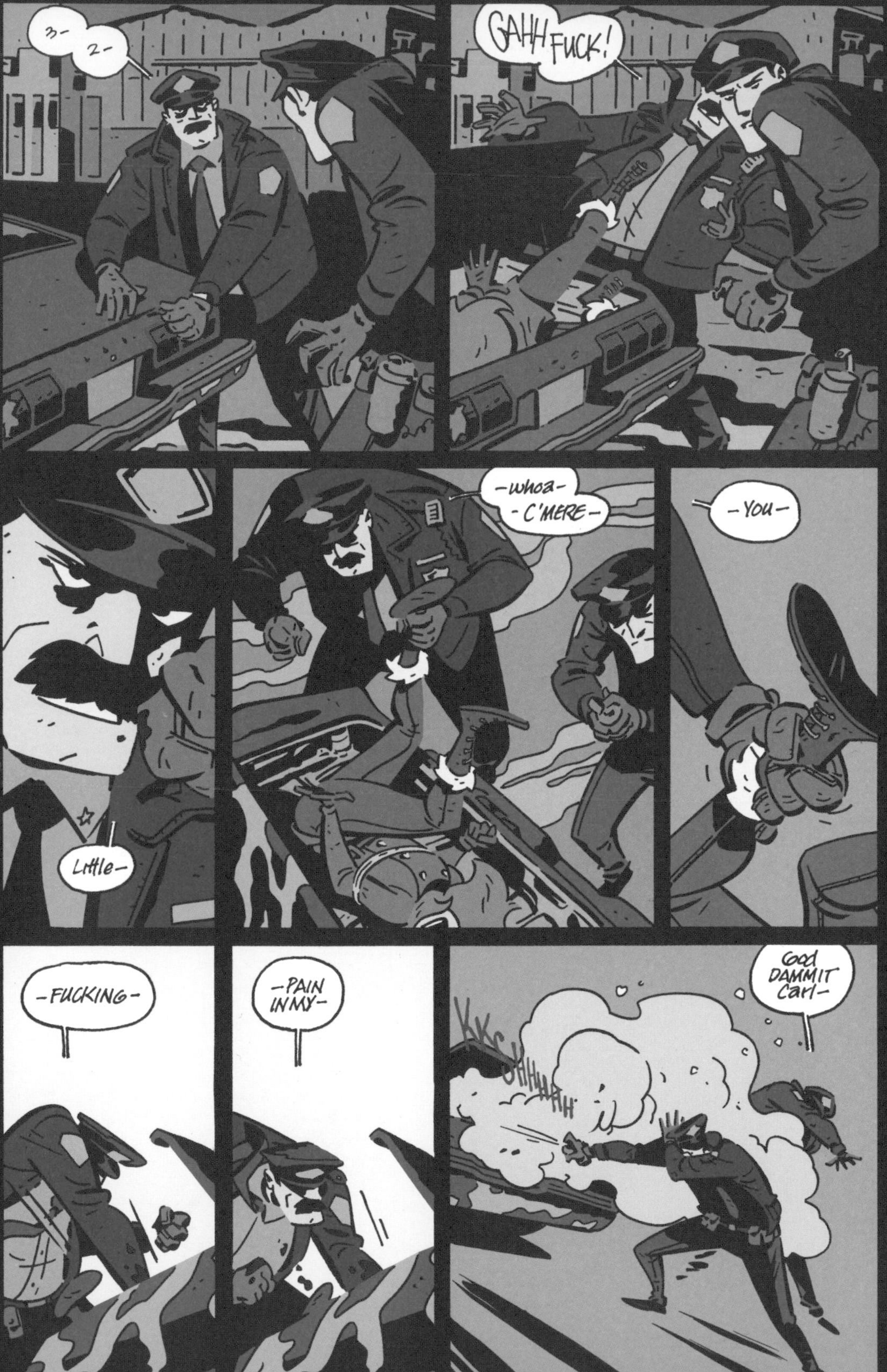
3-
2-
GAHH FUCK!
Little-
-whoa-
C'MERE-
-YOU-
-FUCKING-
-PAIN IN MY-
God DAMMIT Carl-

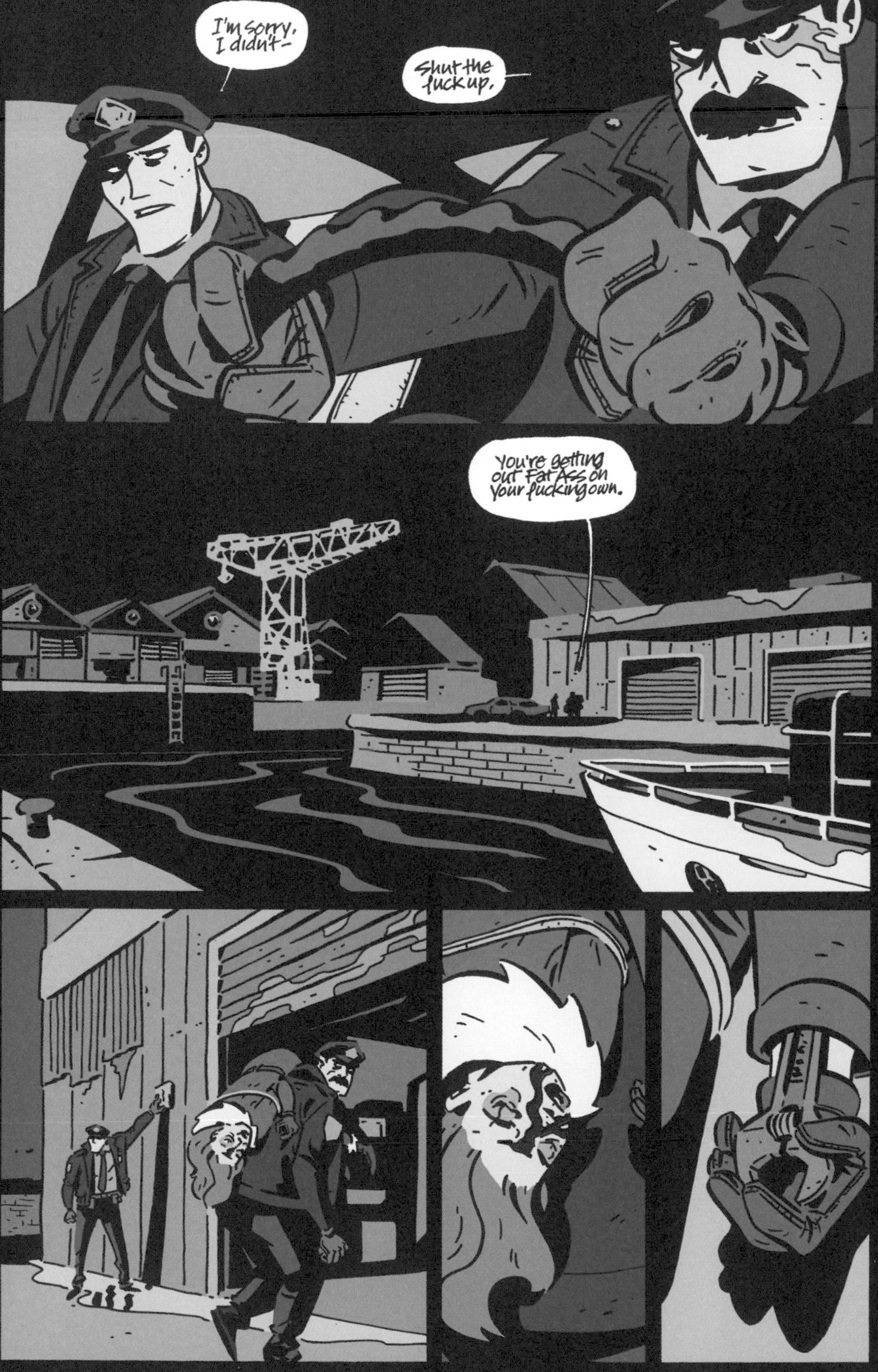
I'm sorry, I didn't-
Shut the fuck up.
You're getting out Fat Ass on your fucking own.

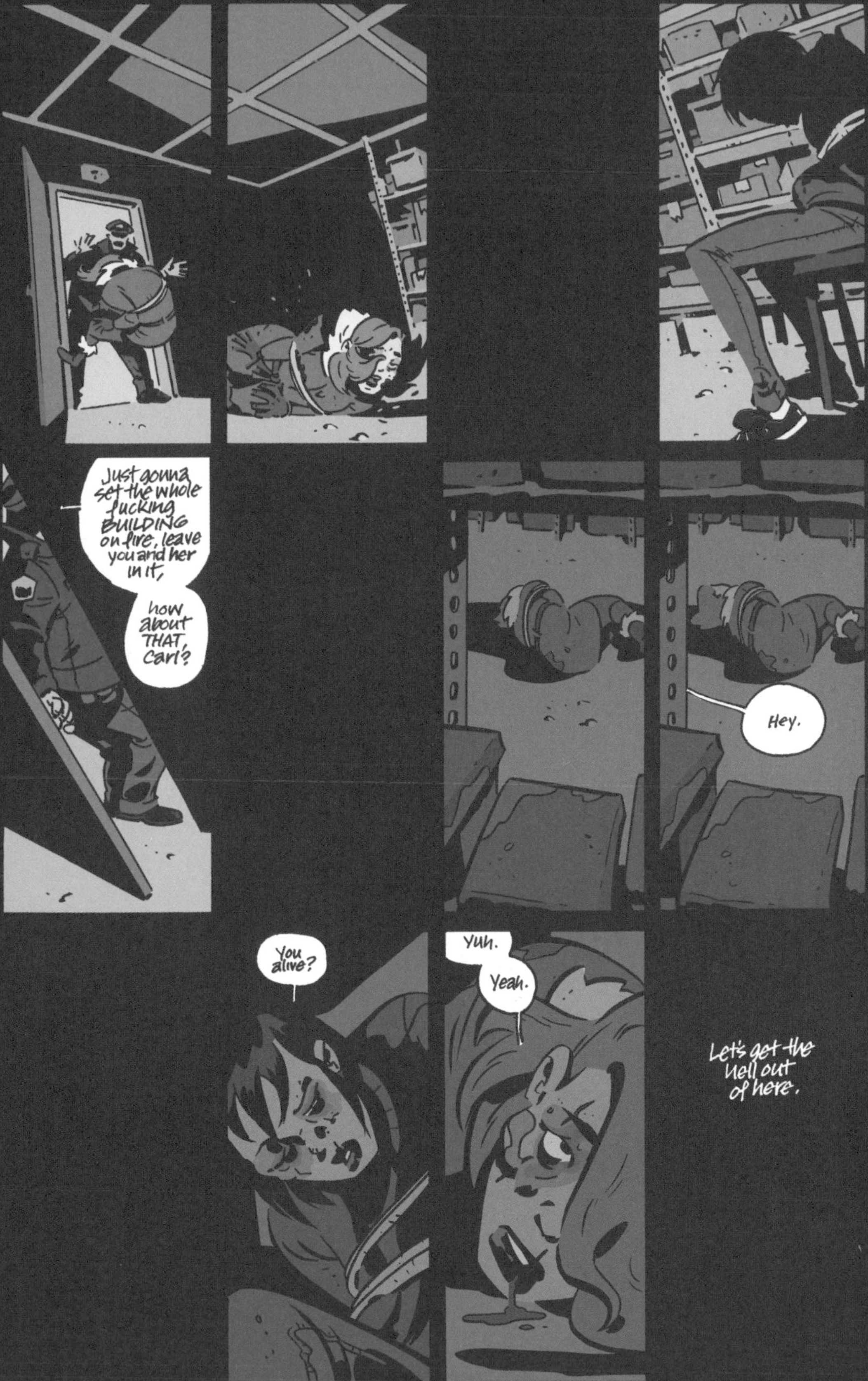
Just gonna set the whole fucking BUILDING on fire, leave you and her in it,
how about THAT, Carl?
Hey.
You alive?
Yuh.
Yeah.
Let's get the hell out of here.

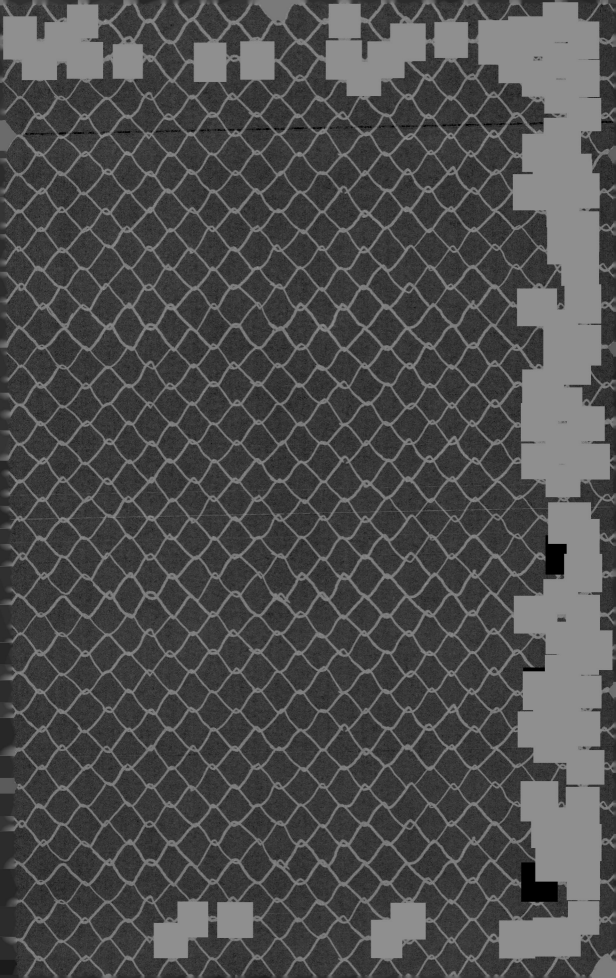

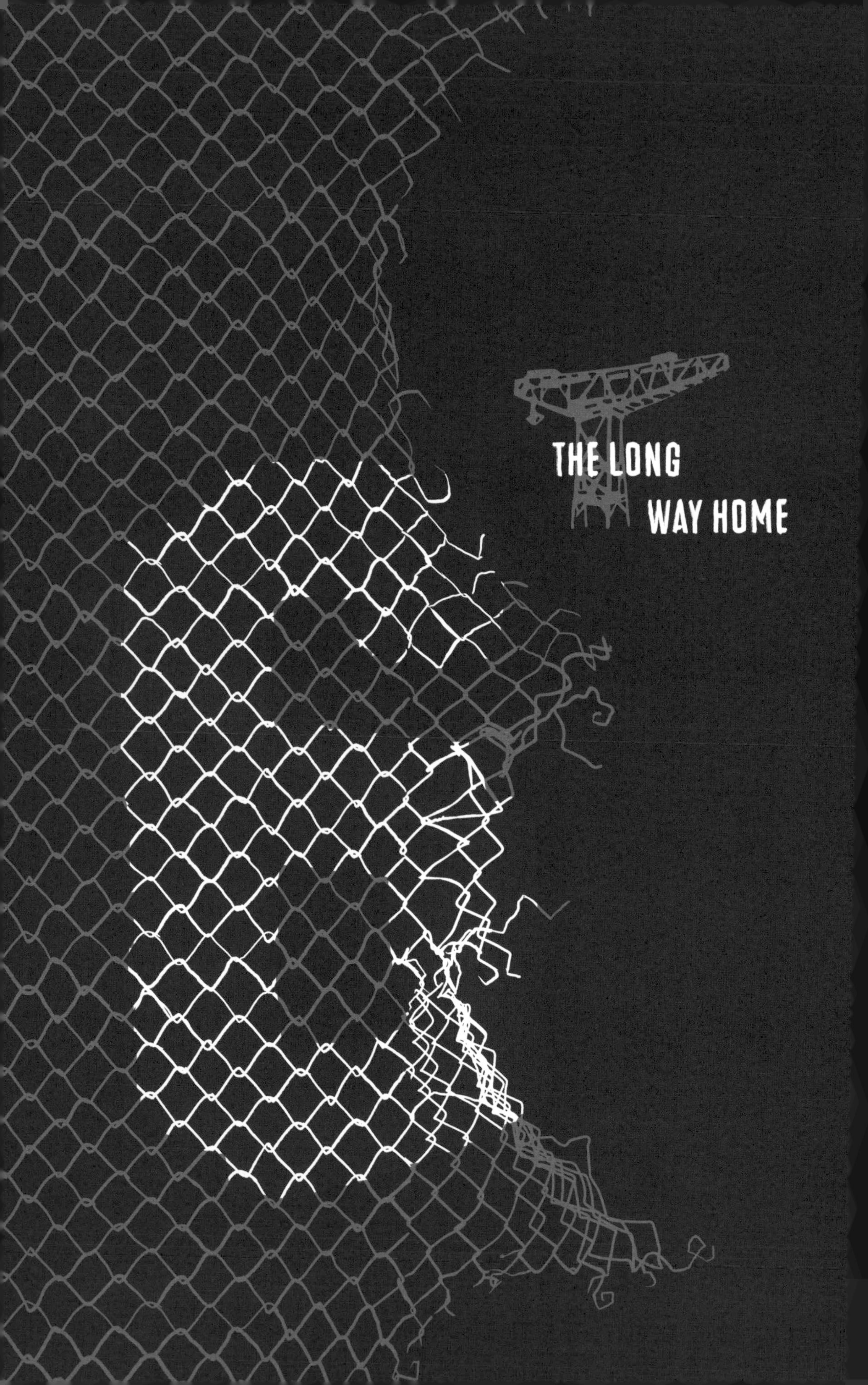
THE LONG
WAY HOME

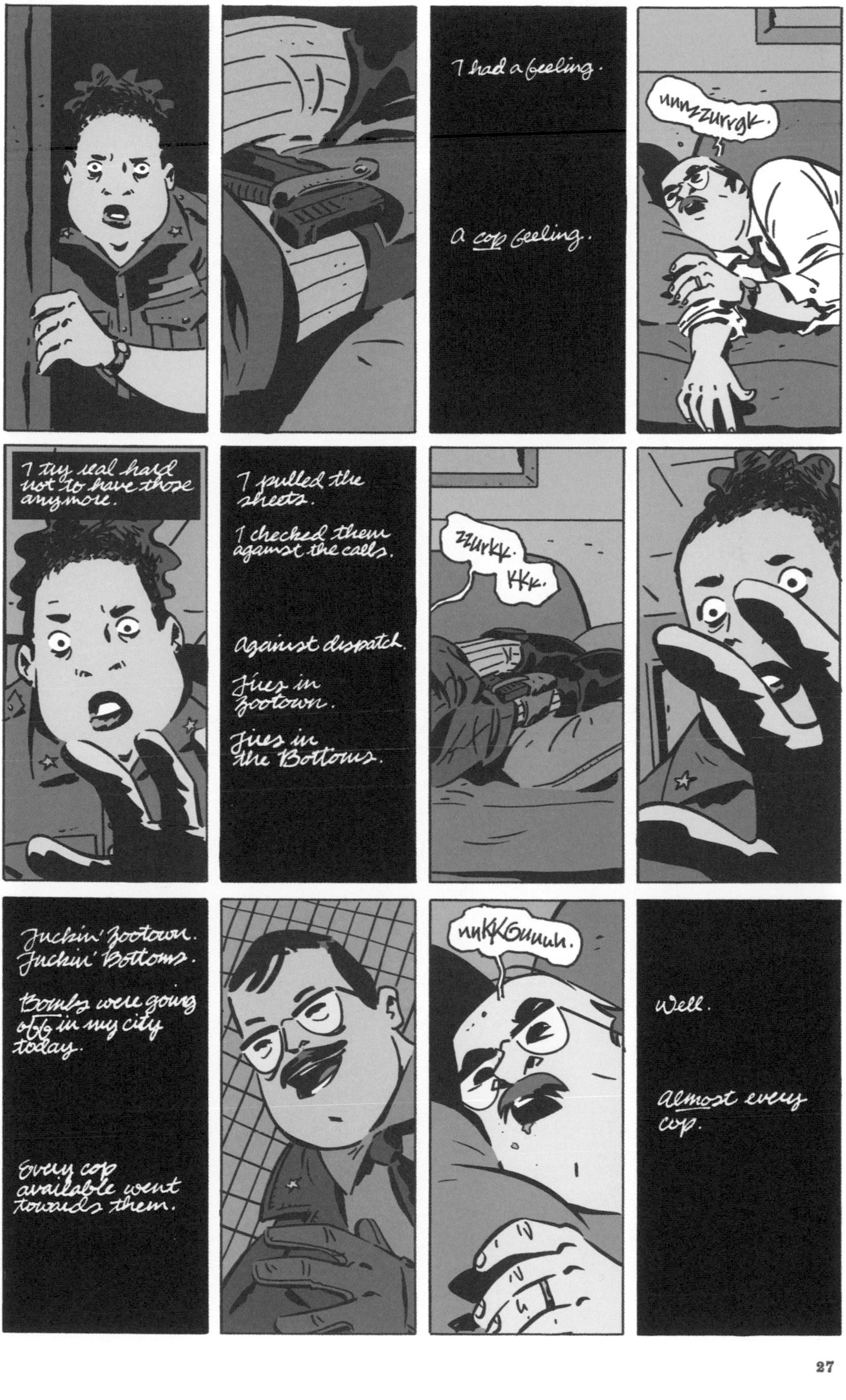
I had a feeling.
A cop feeling.
unnzzurrgk.
I try real hard not to have those anymore.
I pulled the sheets.
I checked them against the calls.
Against dispatch.
Fires in Zootown.
Fires in the Bottoms.
zzurkk.
kkk.
Fuckin' Zootown.
Fuckin' Bottoms.
Bombs were going off in my city today.
Every cop available went towards them.
unnKKGuuuh.
Well.
Almost every cop.

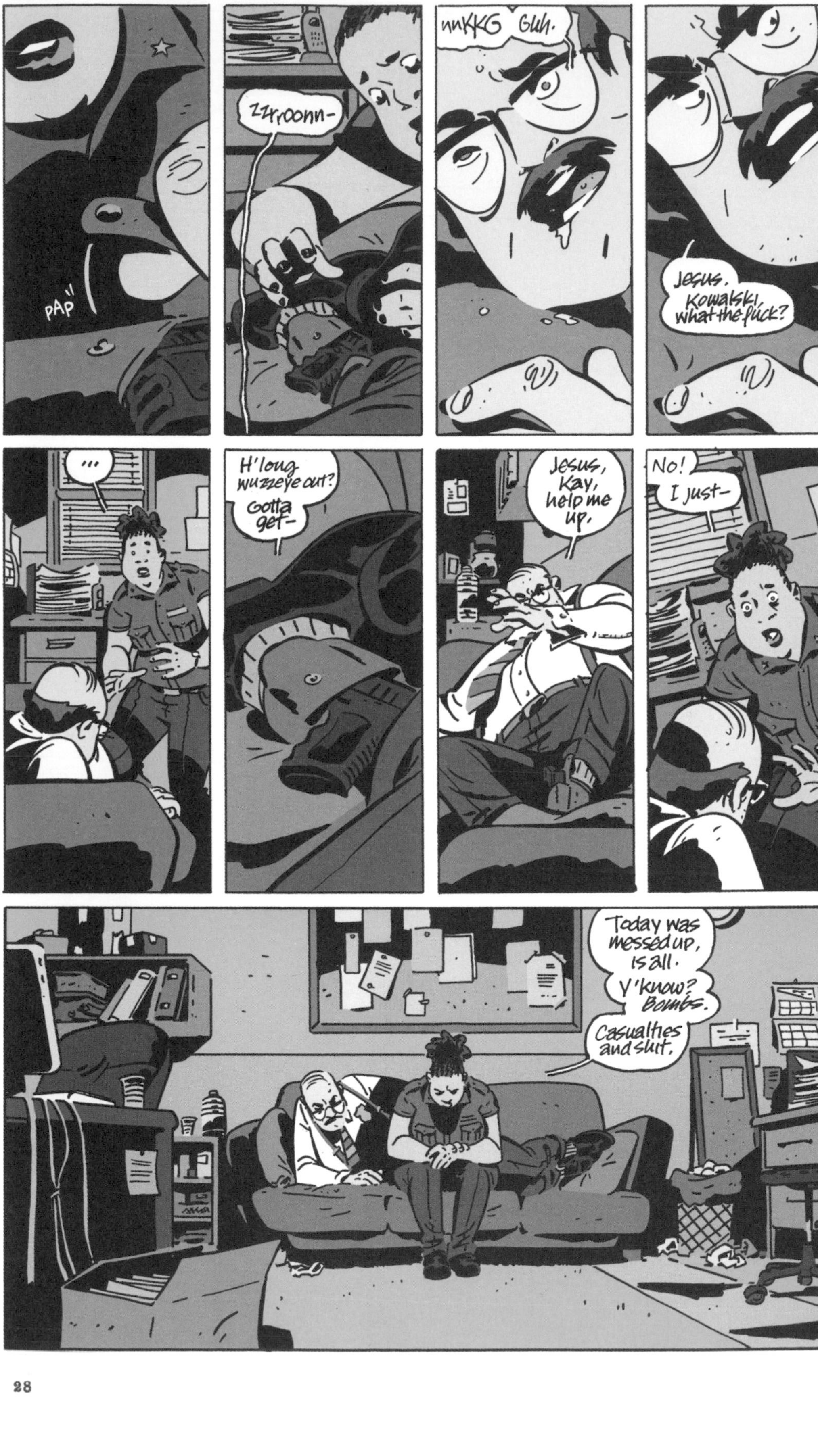
PAP
ZZrroonn-
nnKKG Guh.
Jesus. Kowalski, what the fuck?
...
H'long wuzzeye out?
Gotta get-
Jesus, Kay, help me up.
No! I just-
Today was messed up, is all.
Y'know? Bombs.
Casualties and shit.

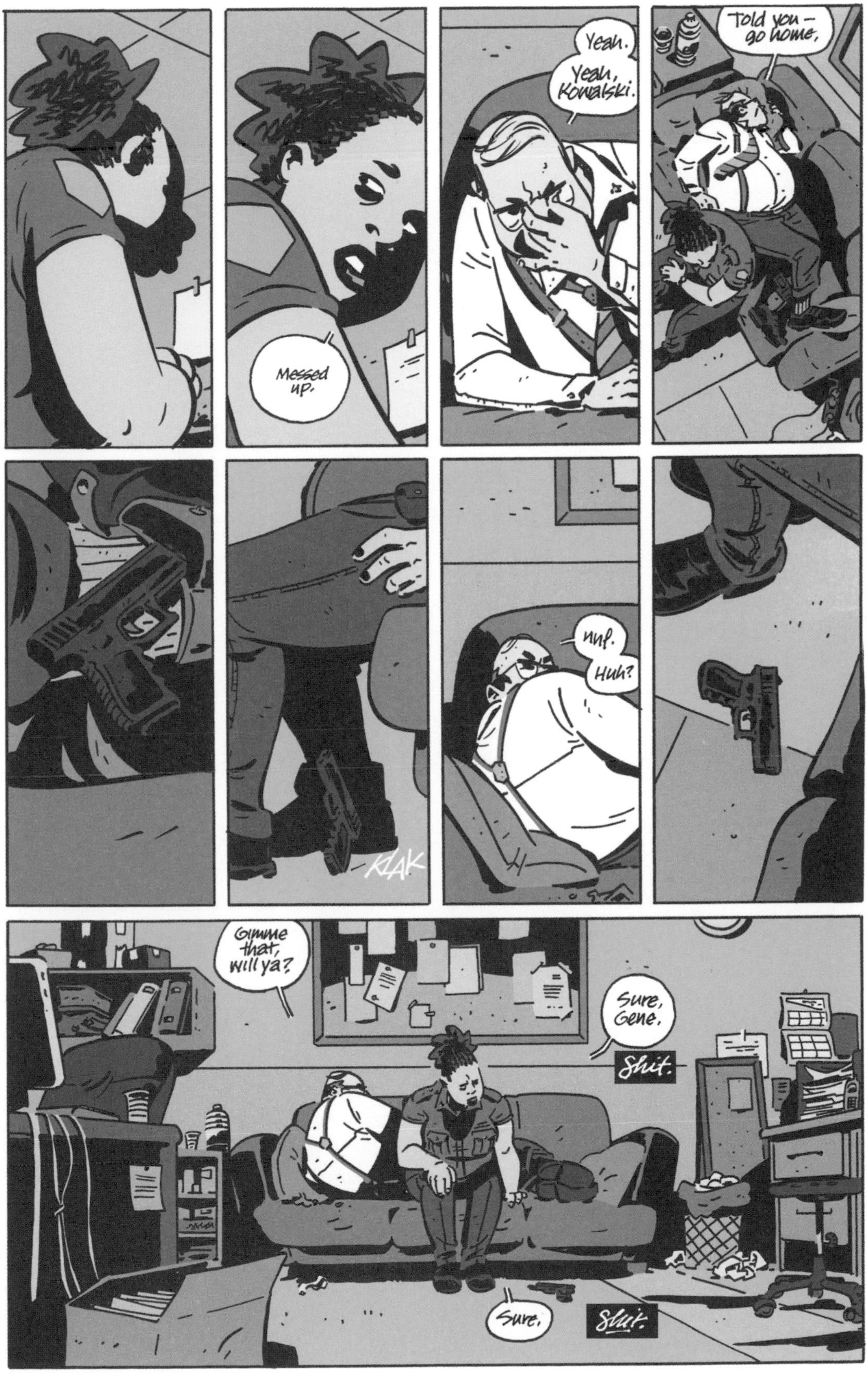
Messed up.
Yeah.
Yeah, Kowalski.
Told you— go home.
KLAK
nnf.
Huh?
Gimme that, will ya?
Sure, Gene.
Shit.
Sure.
Shit.

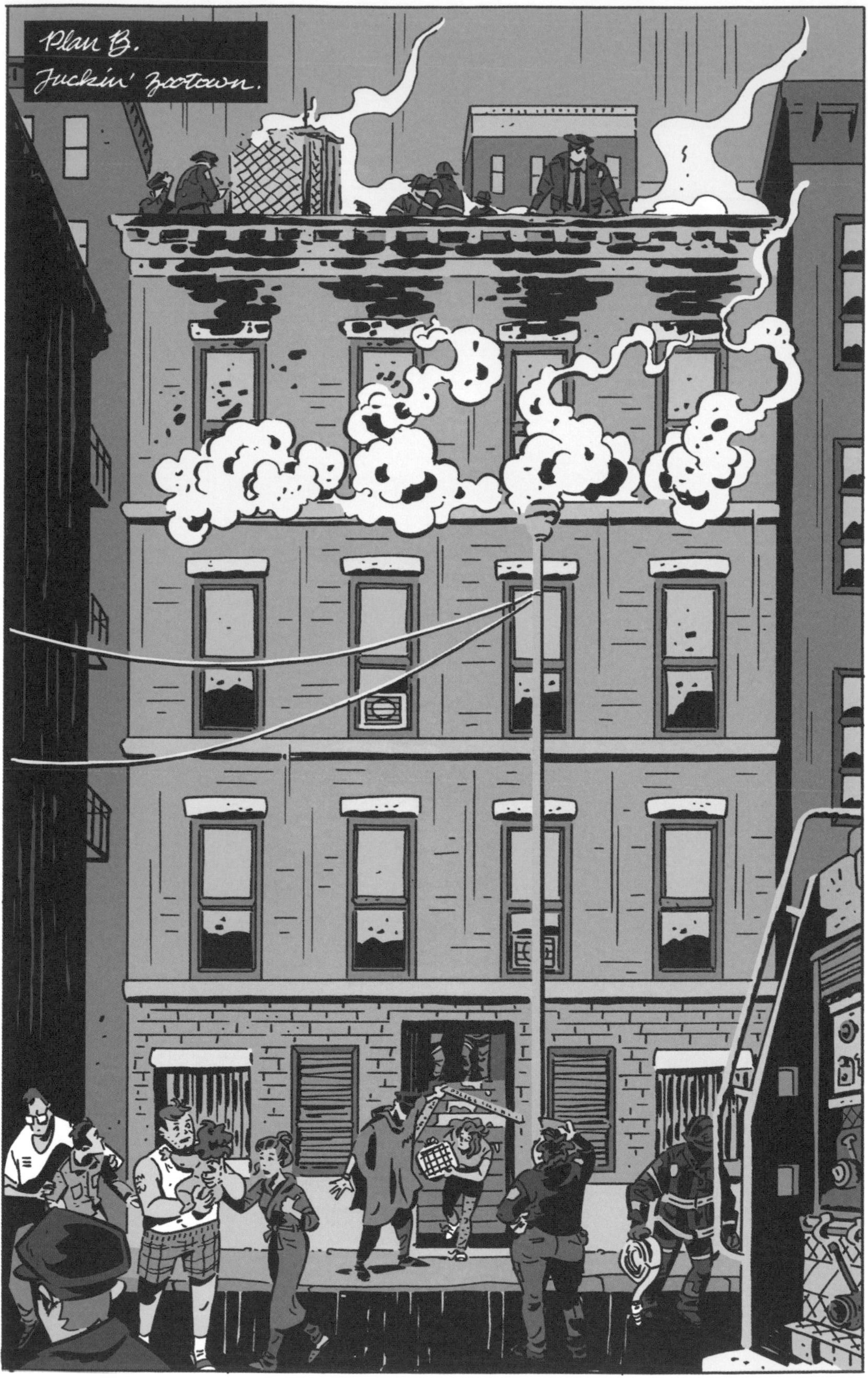
Plan B.
Fuckin' Zootown.

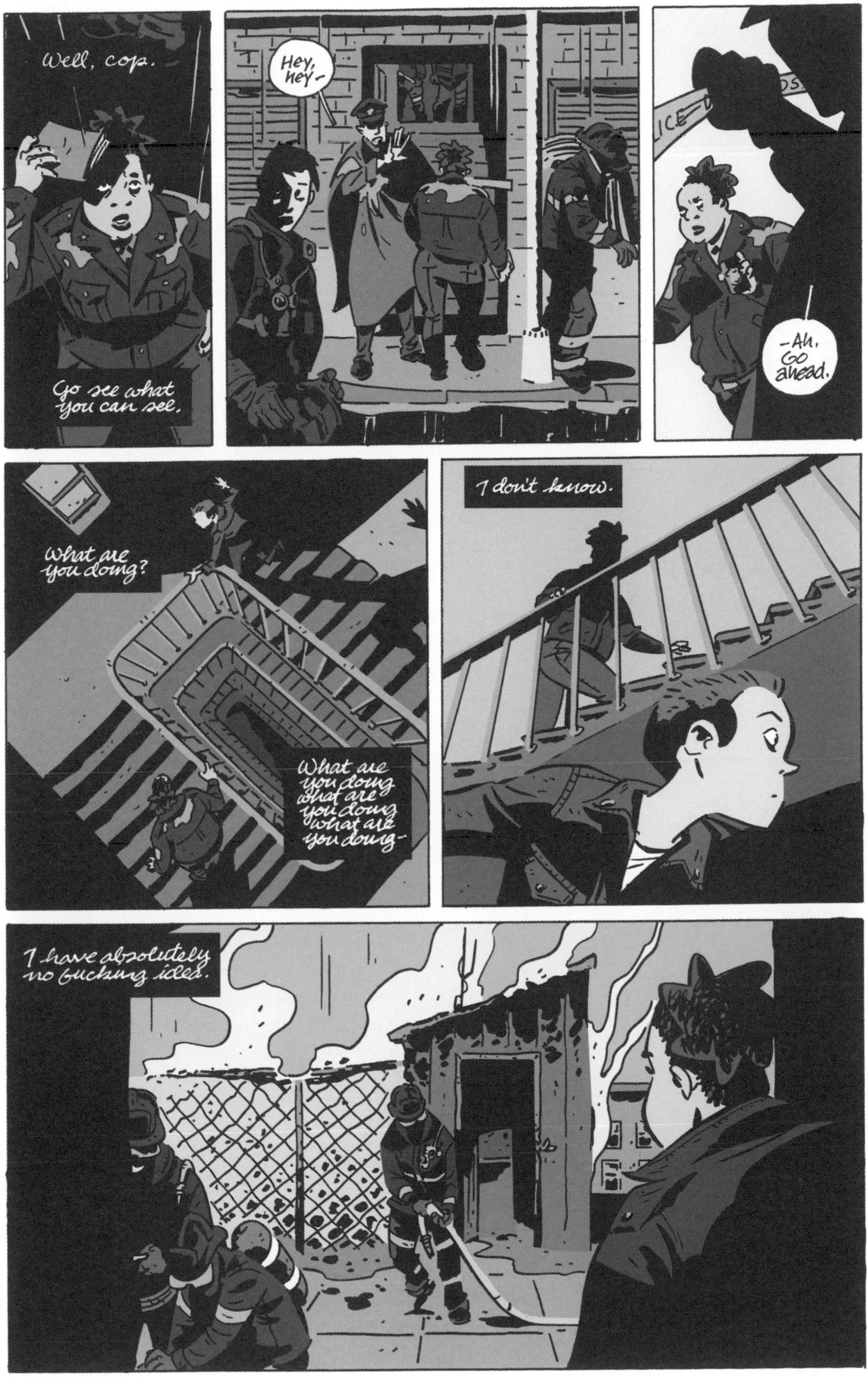
Well, cop.
Go see what you can see.
Hey, hey-
-Ah. Go ahead.
What are you doing?
What are you doing what are you doing what are you doing-
I don't know.
I have absolutely no fucking idea.

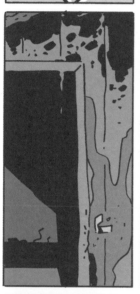

I know what this is.

I know what this was...

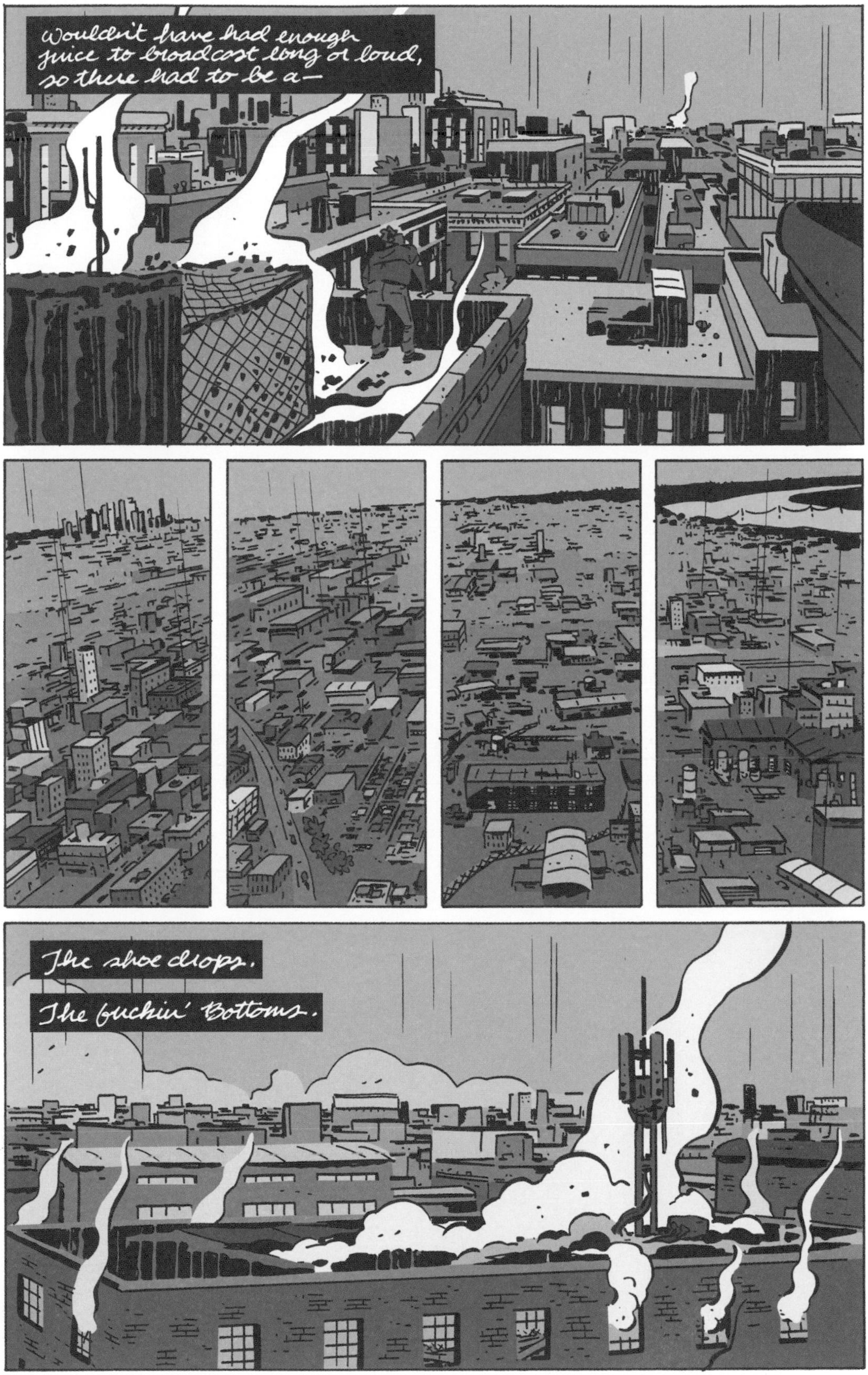
Wouldn't have had enough juice to broadcast long or loud, so there had to be a—
The shoe drops.
The fuckin' Bottoms.

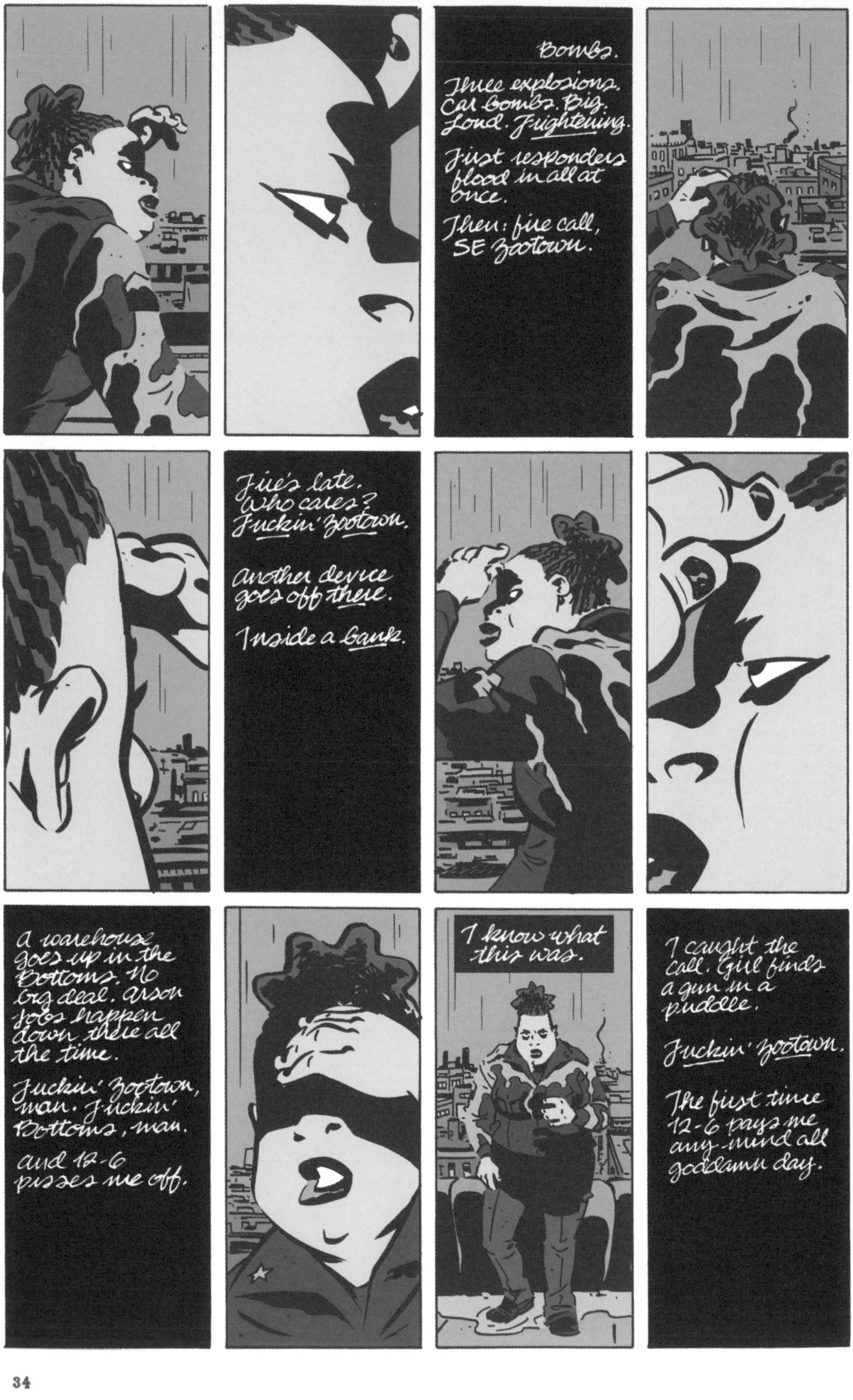
Bombs.
Three explosions. Car bombs. Big. Loud. Frightening.
First responders flood in all at once.
Then: fire call, SE Zootown.
Fire's late. Who cares? Fuckin' Zootown.
Another device goes off there.
Inside a bank.
A warehouse goes up in the Bottoms. No big deal. Arson jobs happen down there all the time.
Fuckin' Zootown, man. Fuckin' Bottoms, man.
And 12-6 pisses me off.
I know what this was.
I caught the call. Girl finds a gun in a puddle.
Fuckin' Zootown.
The first time 12-6 pays me any mind all goddamn day.

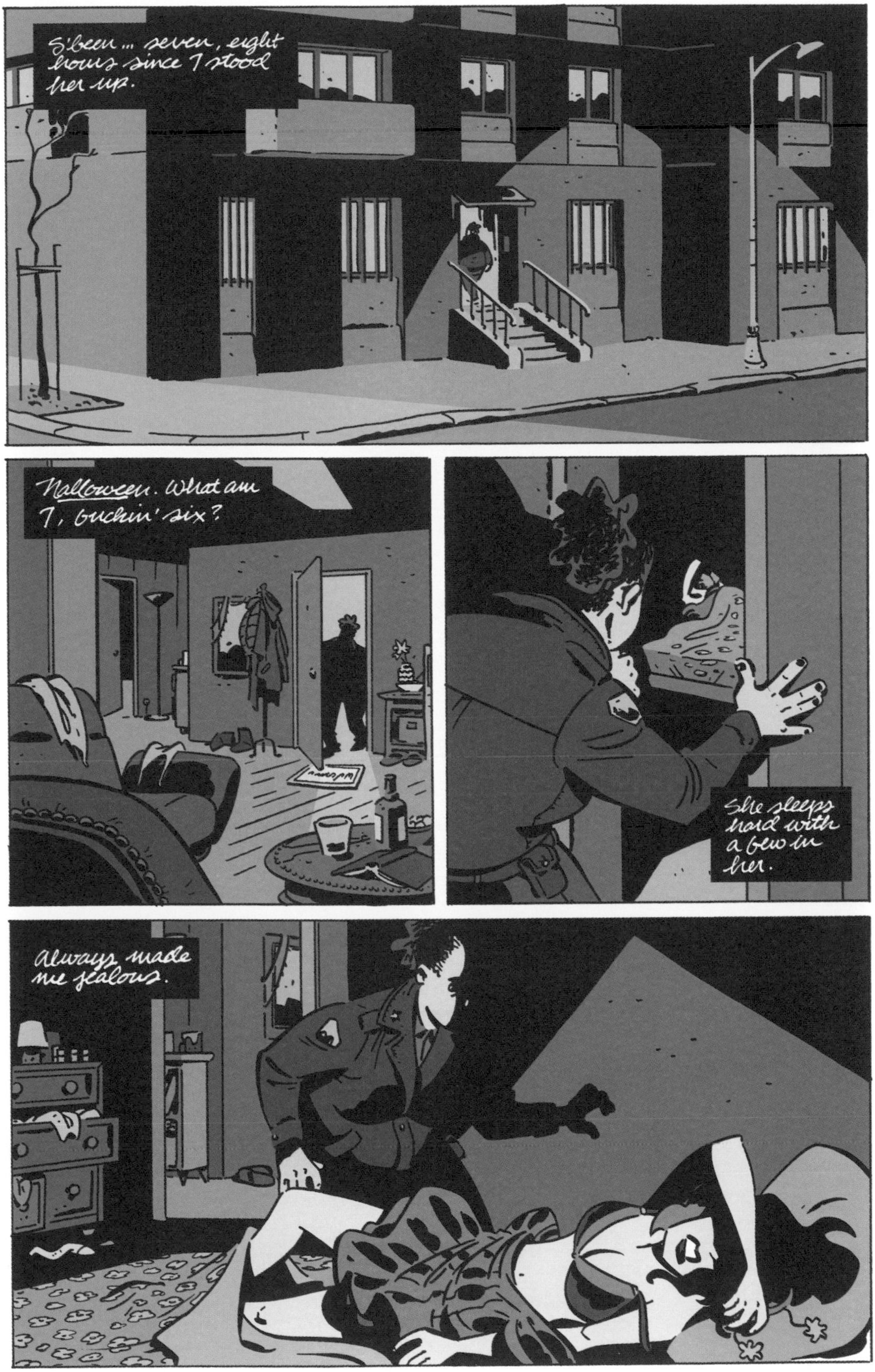
S'been... seven, eight hours since I stood her up.
Halloween. What am I, fuckin' six?
She sleeps hard with a few in her.
Always made me jealous.

come on...

zzzyk
Ook
zkk

Kayzatyuhh...

I lean down, like a trapped animal.

I move my hand until I find what I need.

I'm sorry, baby.

I'm so sorry for everything.

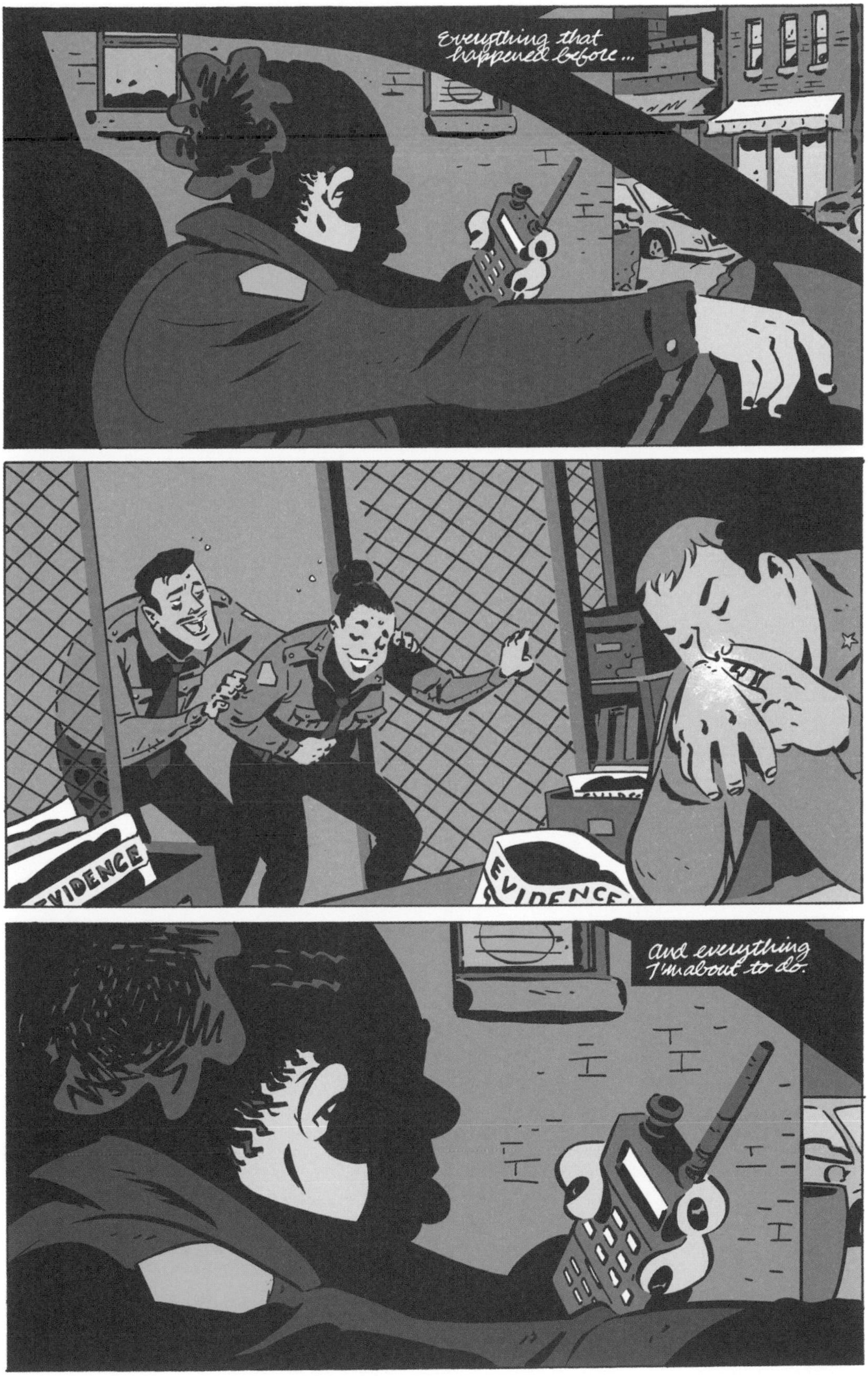
Everything that happened before...
EVIDENCE
and everything I'm about to do.

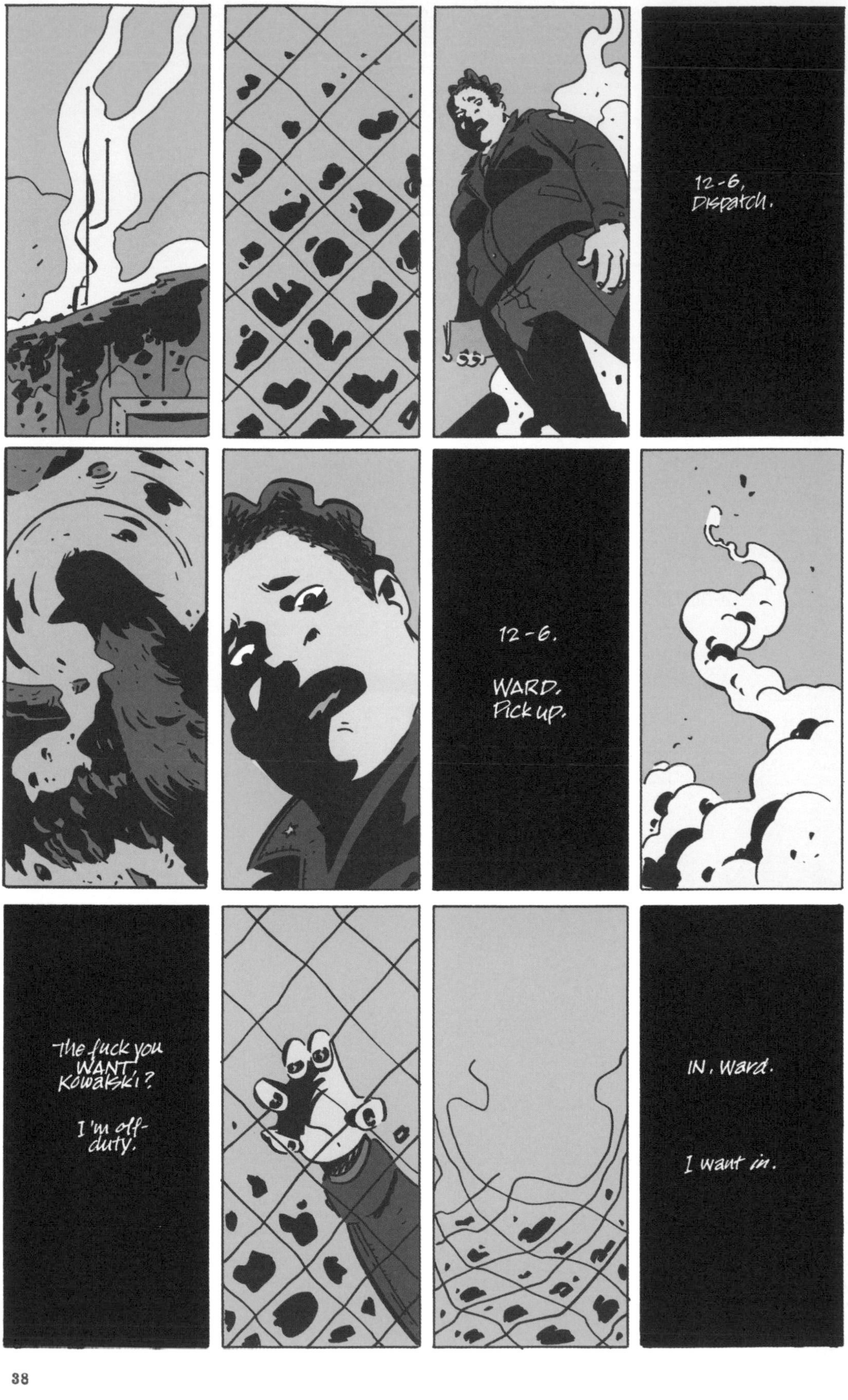
12-6, Dispatch.
12-6.
WARD. Pick up.
The fuck you WANT, Kowalski?
I'm off-duty.
IN. Ward.
I want in.

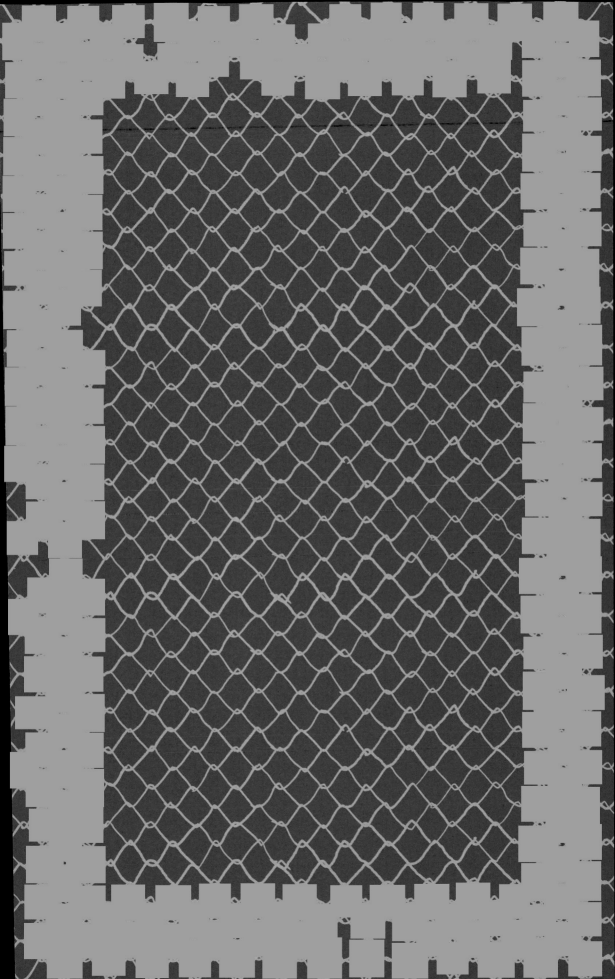

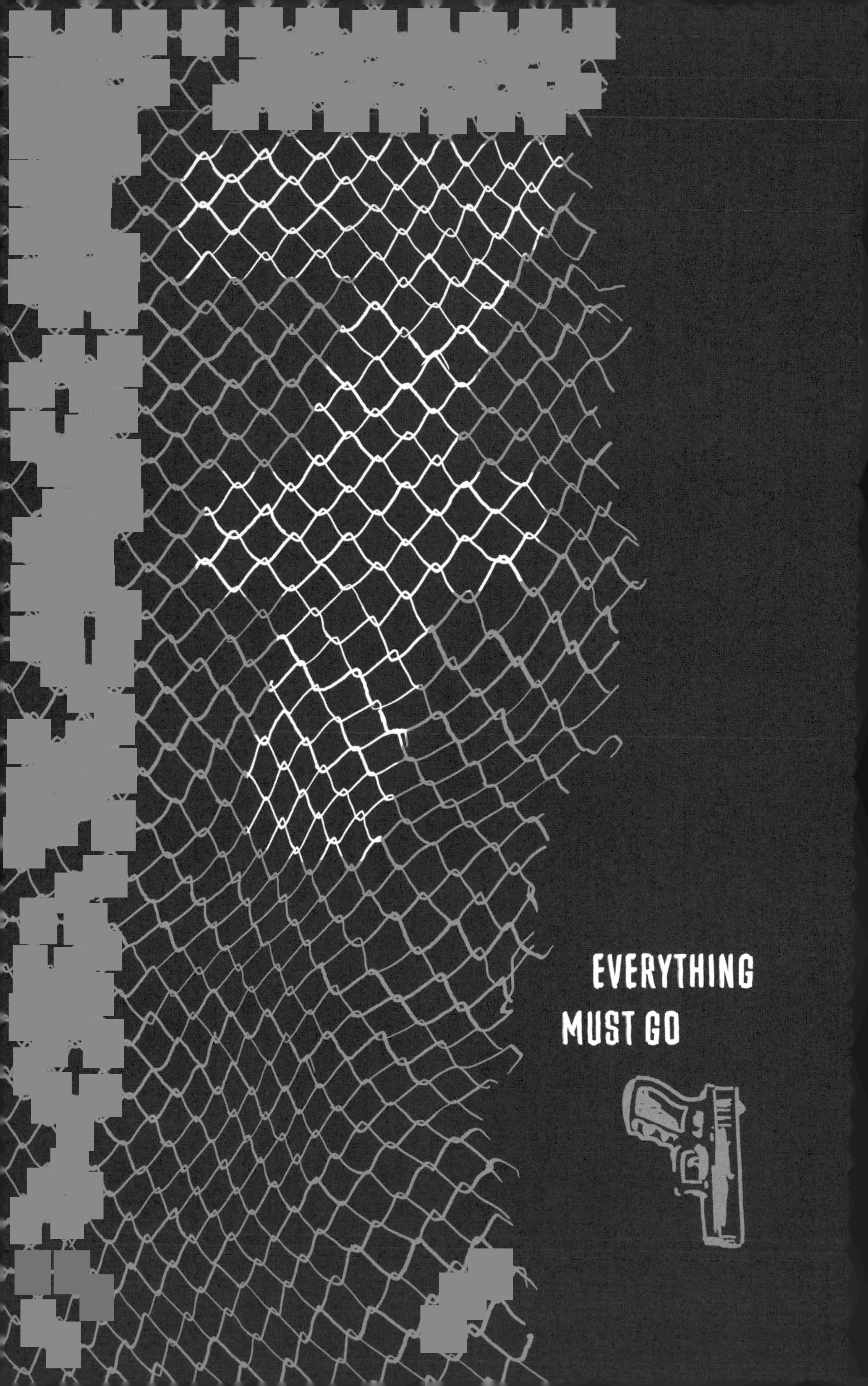
EVERYTHING
MUST GO

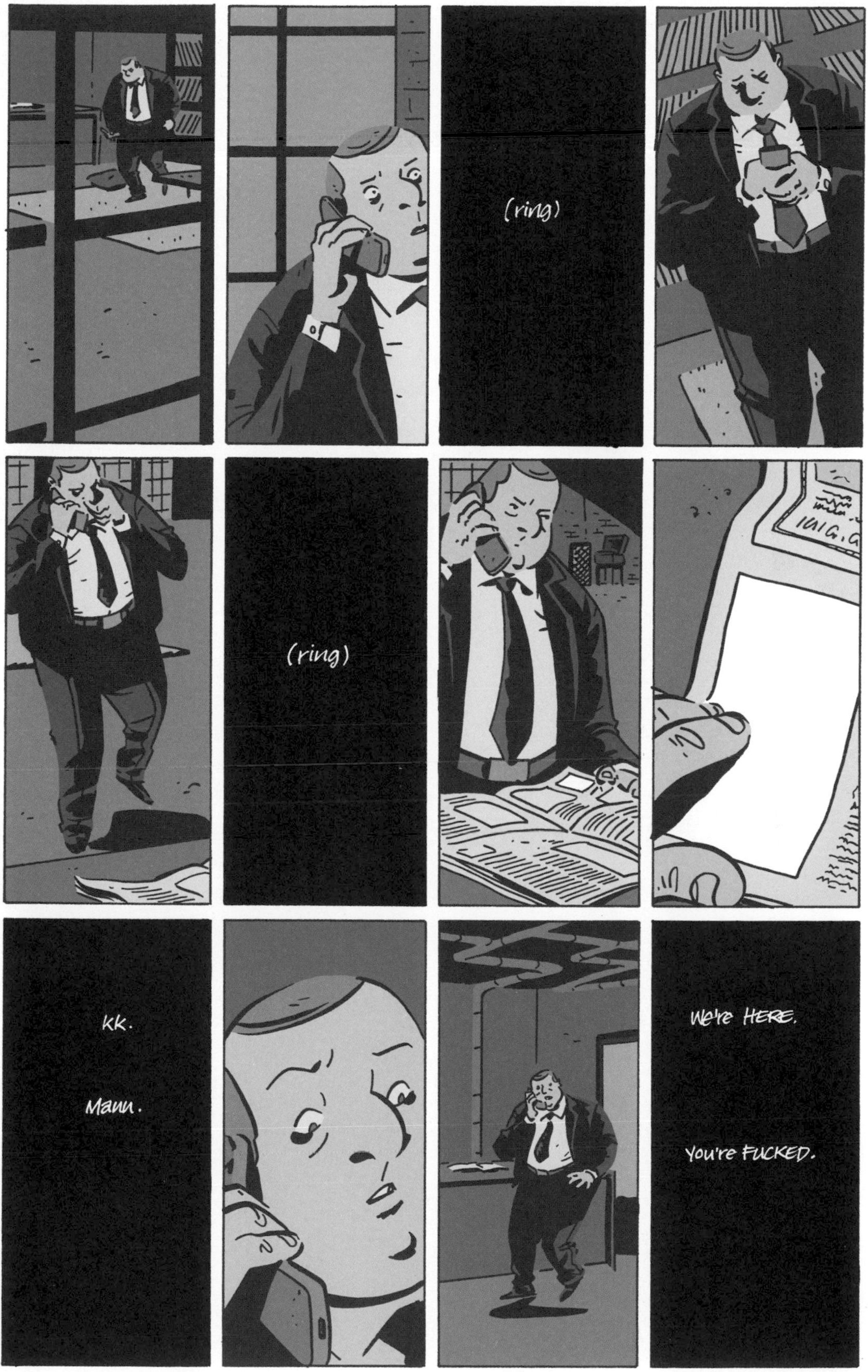
(ring)
(ring)
kk.
Mann.
We're HERE.
You're FUCKED.

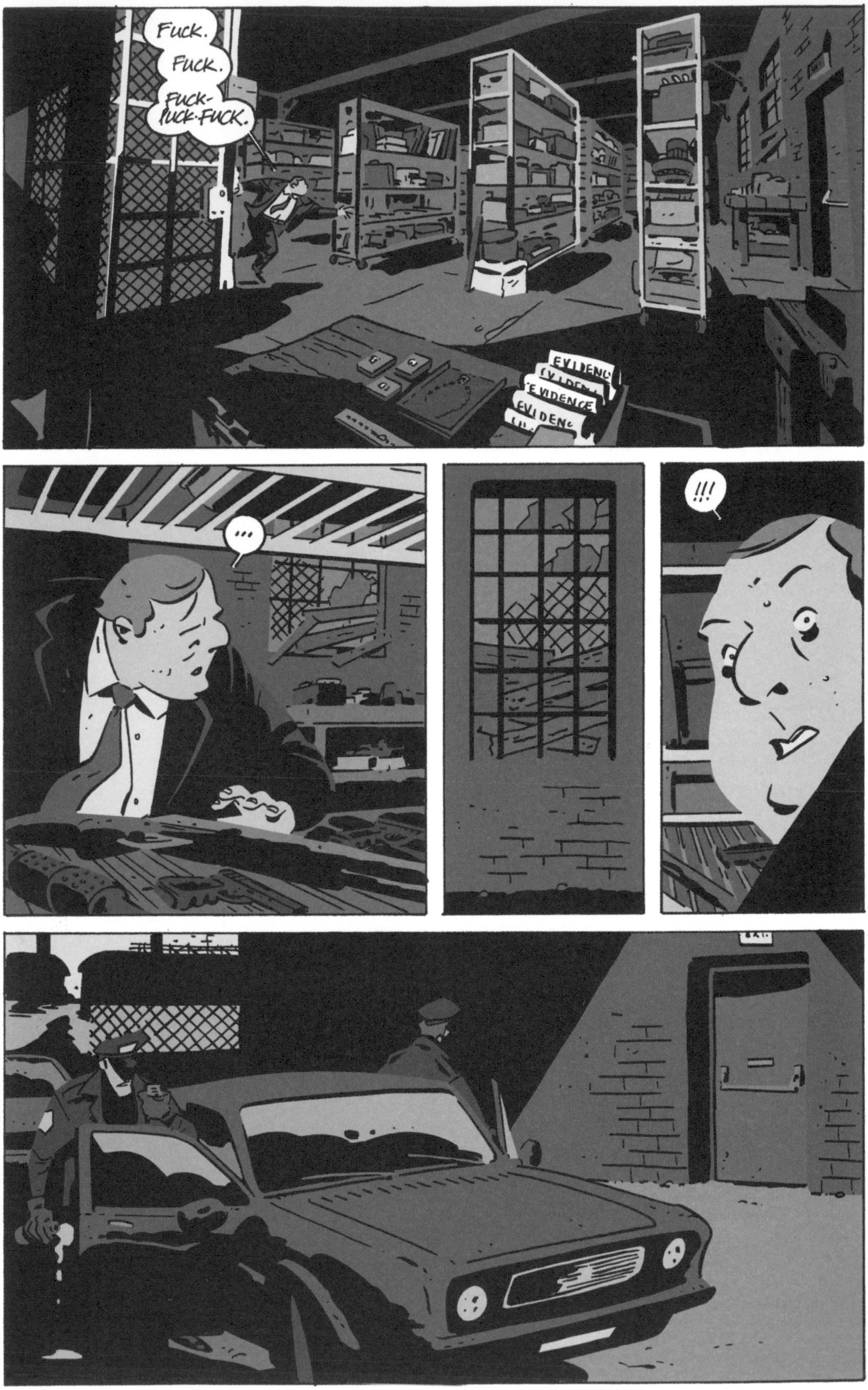
FUCK.
FUCK.
FUCK-FUCK-FUCK.
EVIDENCE
...
!!!

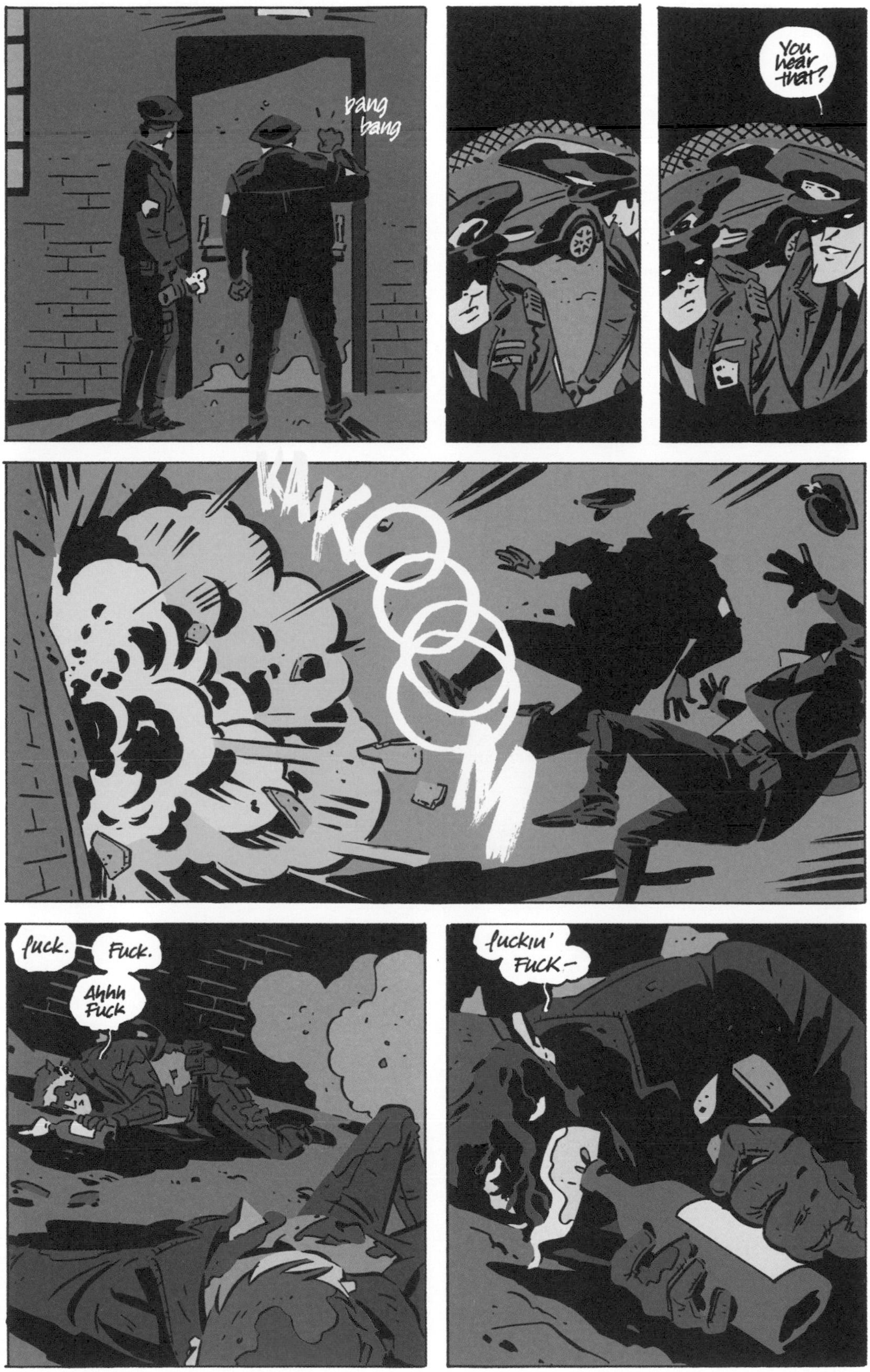
bang
bang
You hear that?
KAKOOOOOM
fuck.
Fuck.
Ahhh Fuck
fuckin' Fuck-

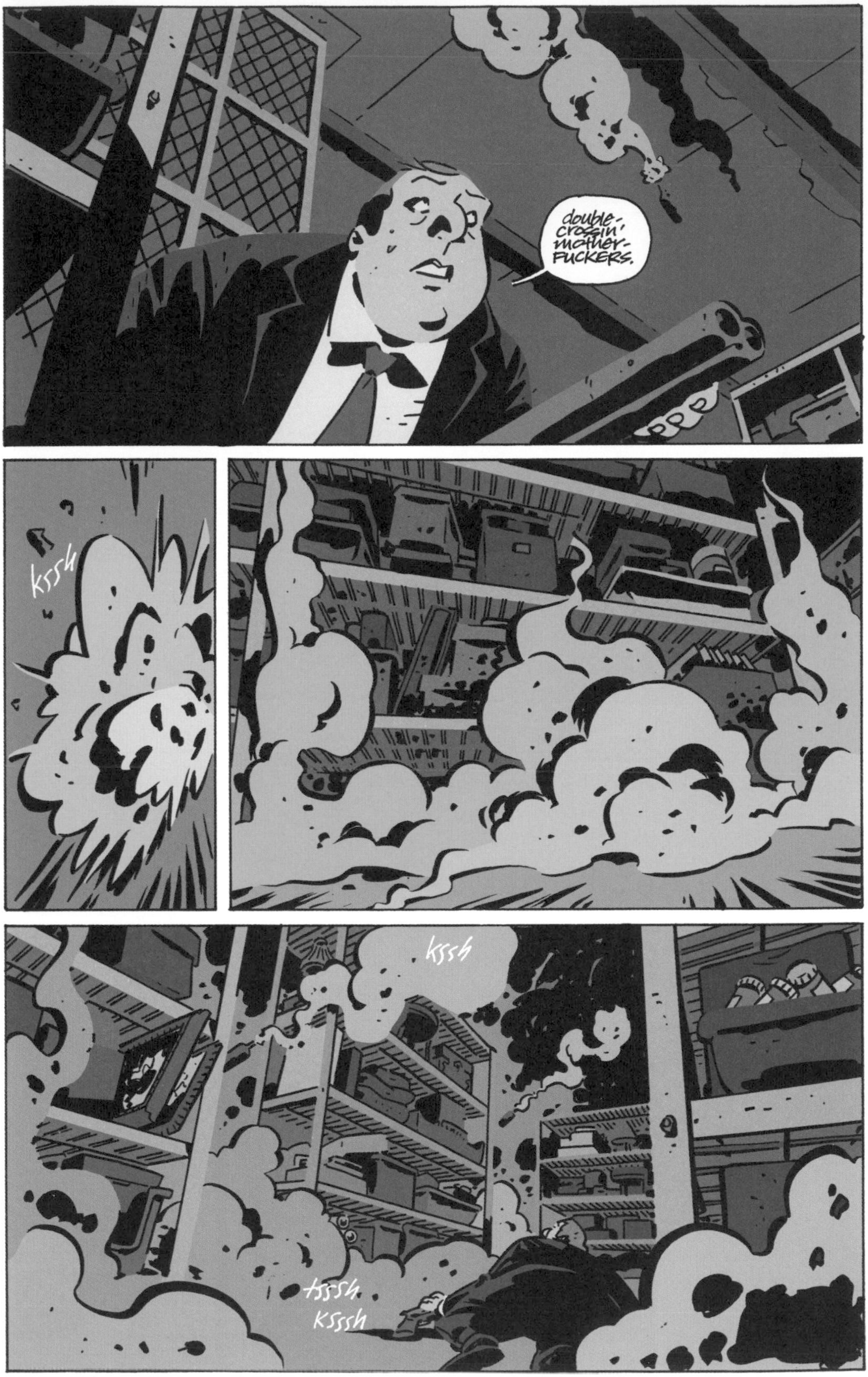
double-crossin' mother-FUCKERS.
kssh
kssh
tsssh
kssssh

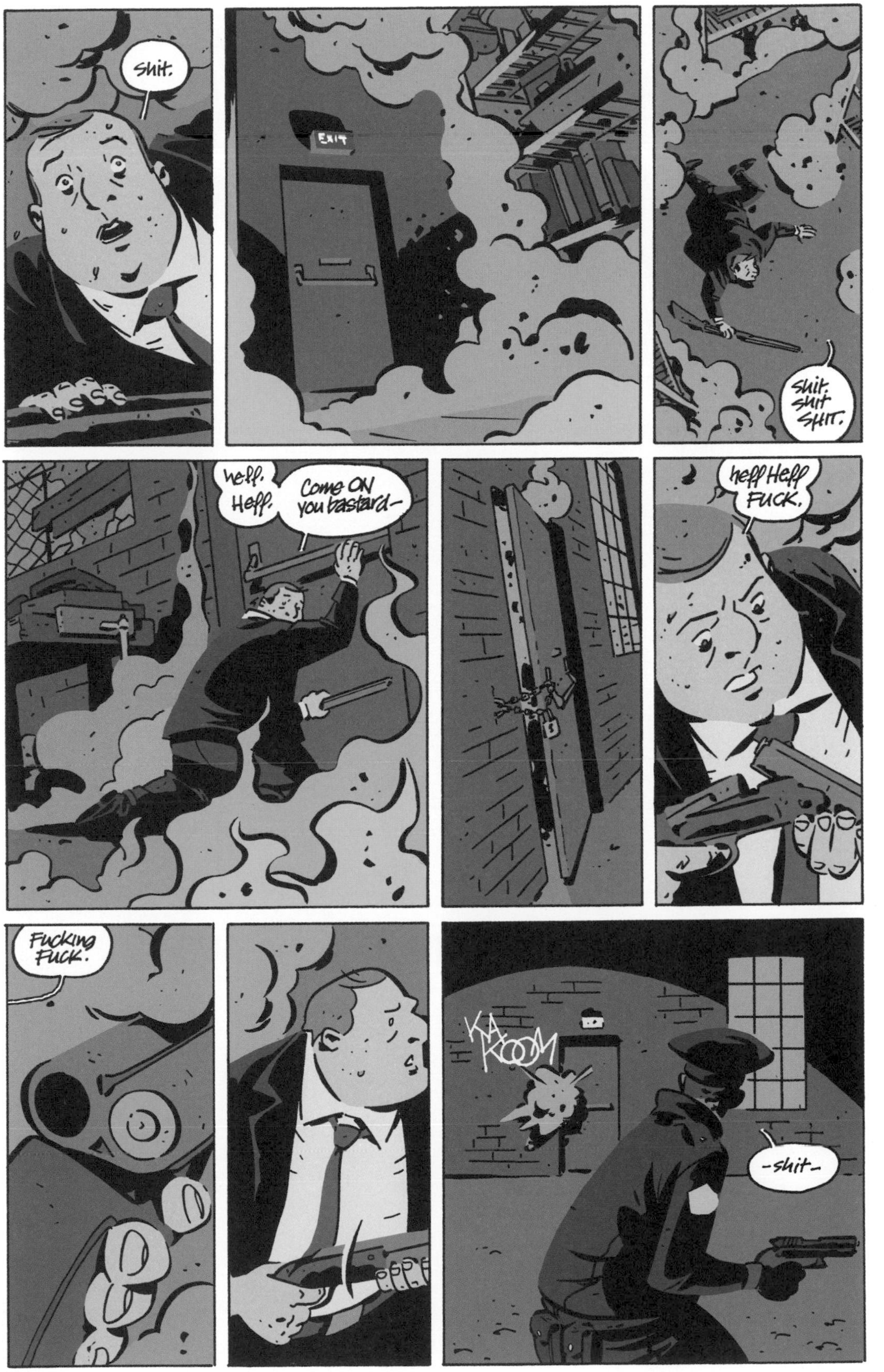
shit.
shit. shit SHIT.
heff. Heff.
Come ON you bastard-
heff Heff FUCK.
Fucking Fuck.
KA KOOM
-shit-

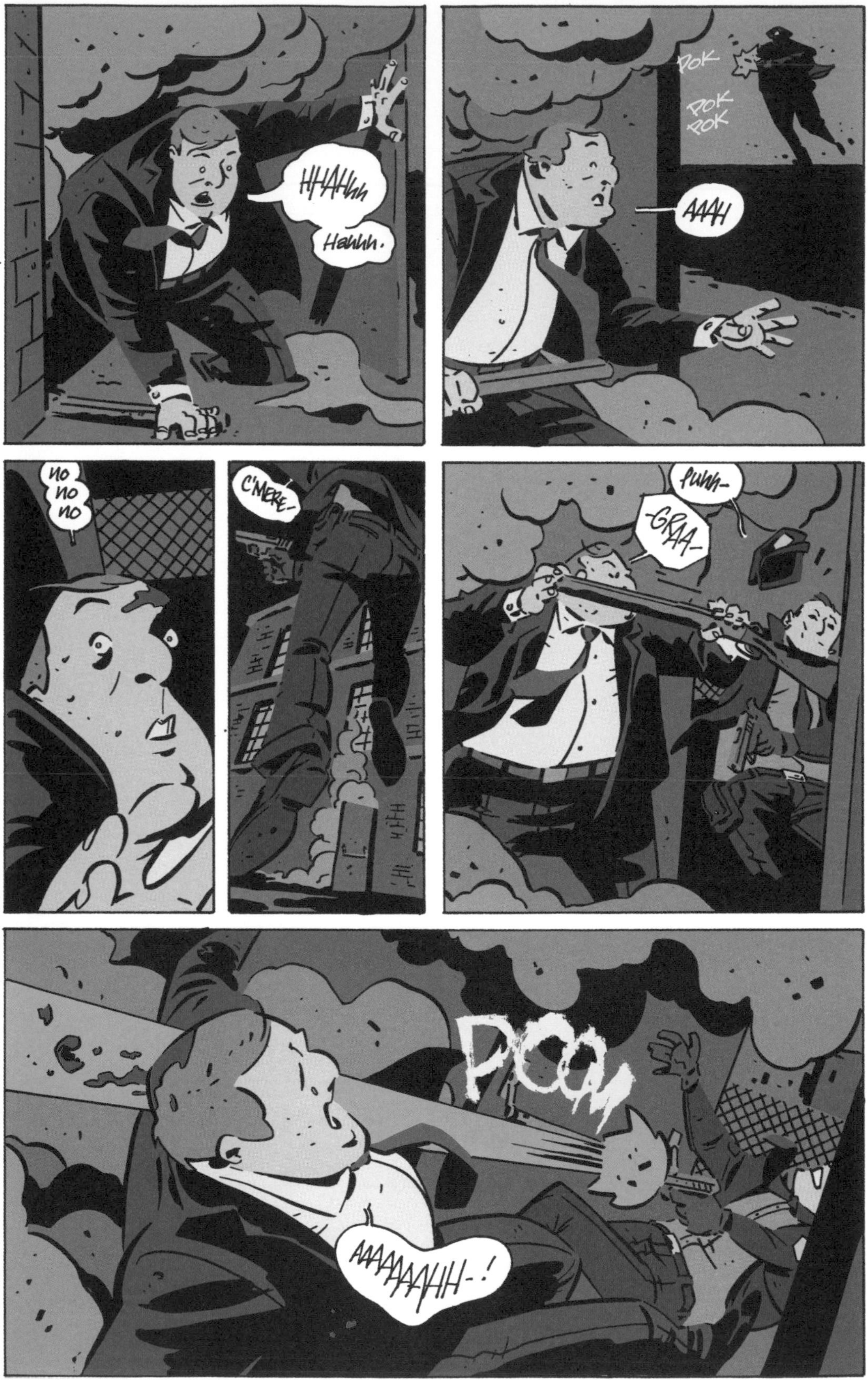
HHAHhh
Hahhh.
POK
POK
POK
AAAH
no
no
no
C'MERE-
Puhh-
-GRAA-
POOM
AAAAAAAHH-.!

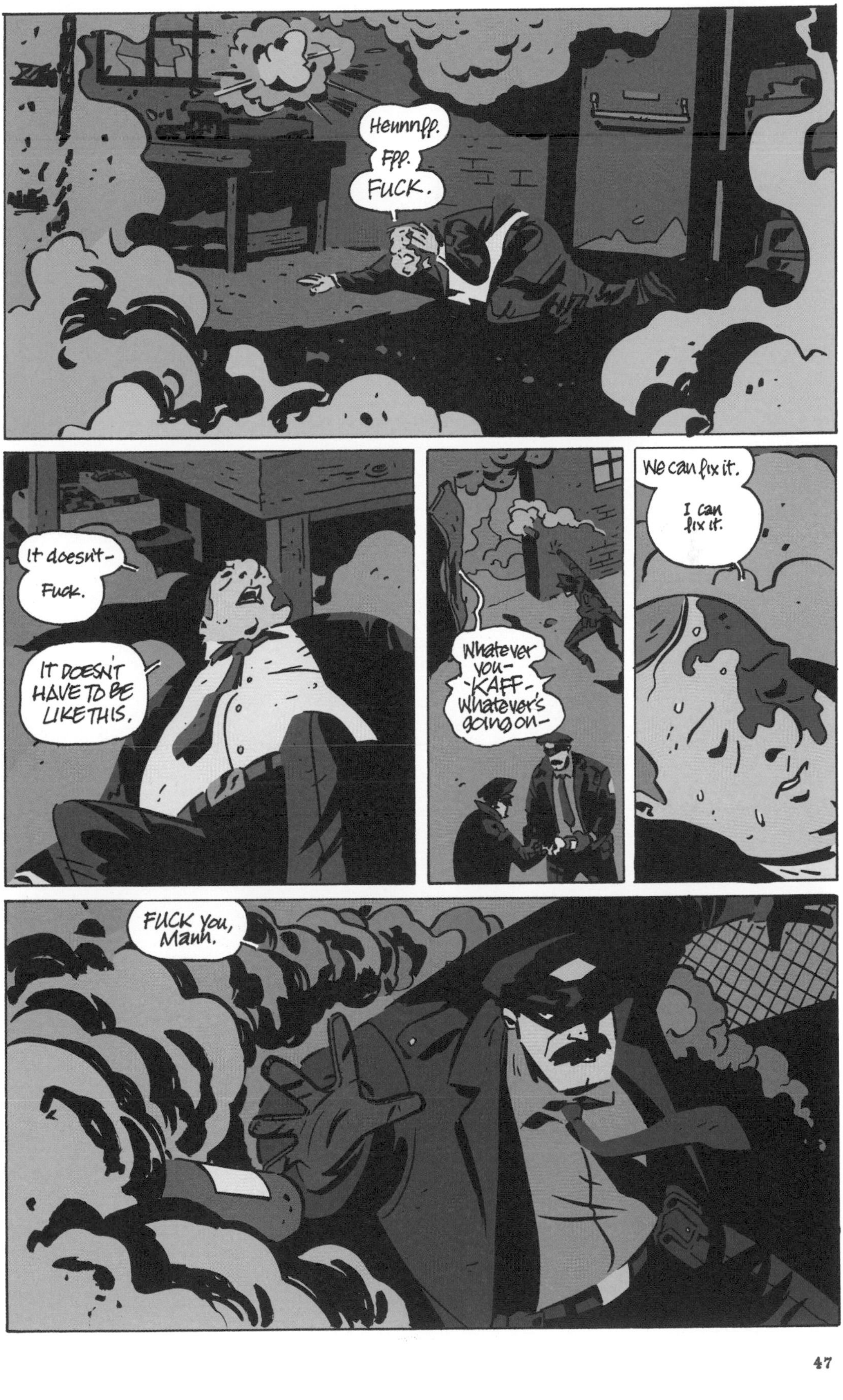
Hennnff. Fff. FUCK.
It doesn't- Fuck.
IT DOESN'T HAVE TO BE LIKE THIS.
Whatever you- -KAFF- Whatever's going on-
We can fix it.
I can fix it.
FUCK you, Mann.

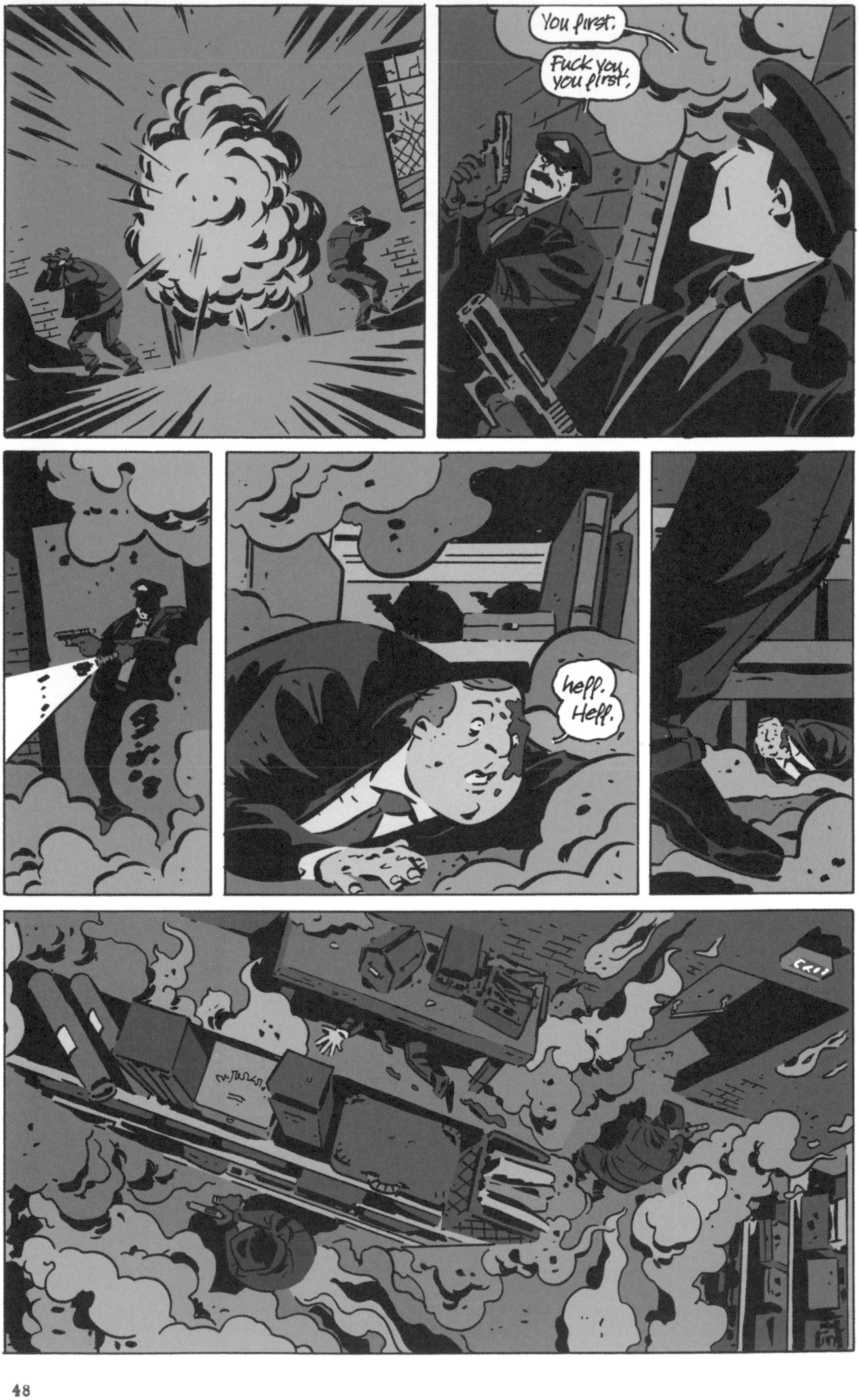
You first.
Fuck you, you first.
hepp. Hepp.

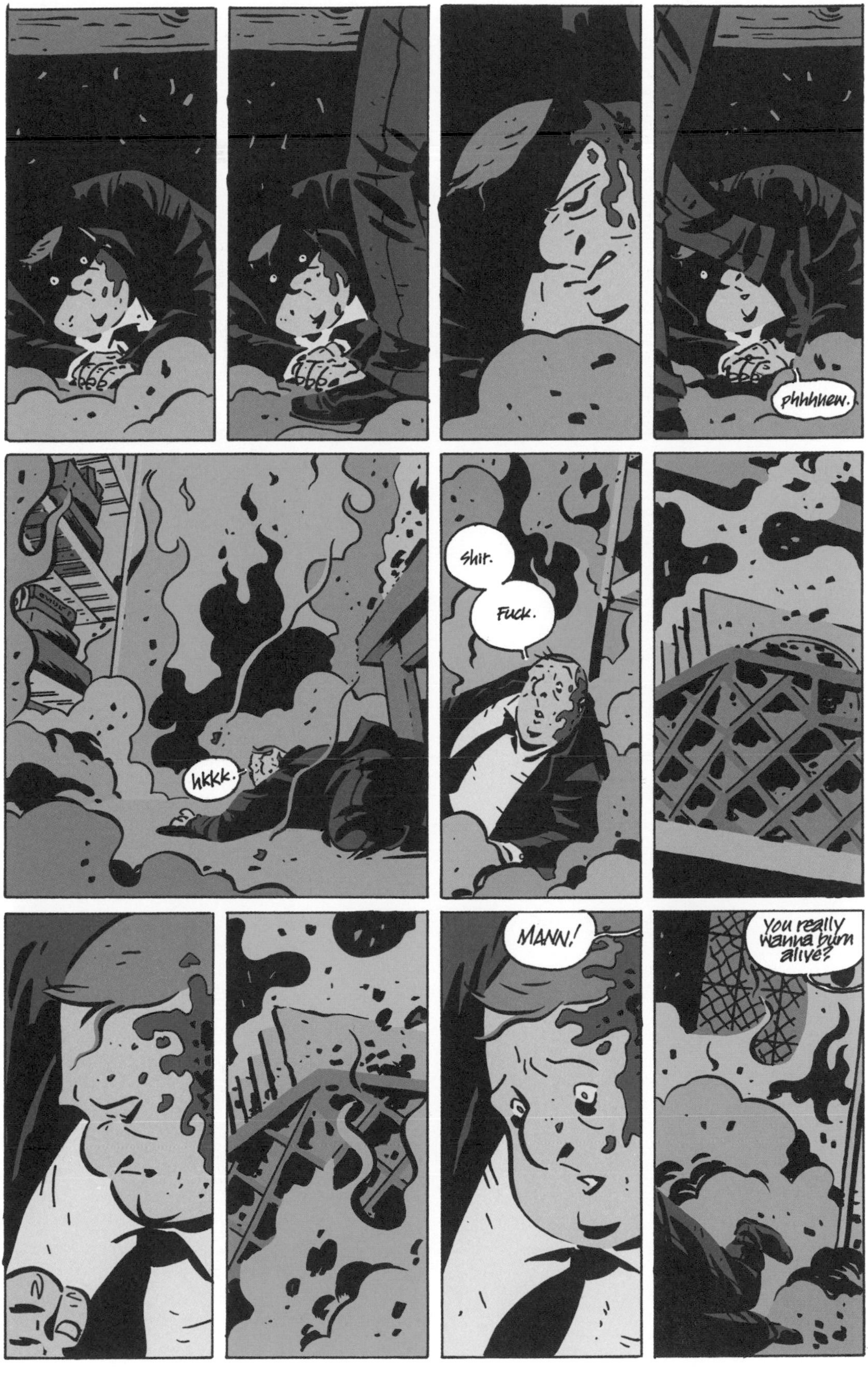
phhhhew.
hkkk.
Shit.
Fuck.
MANN!
You really wanna burn alive?

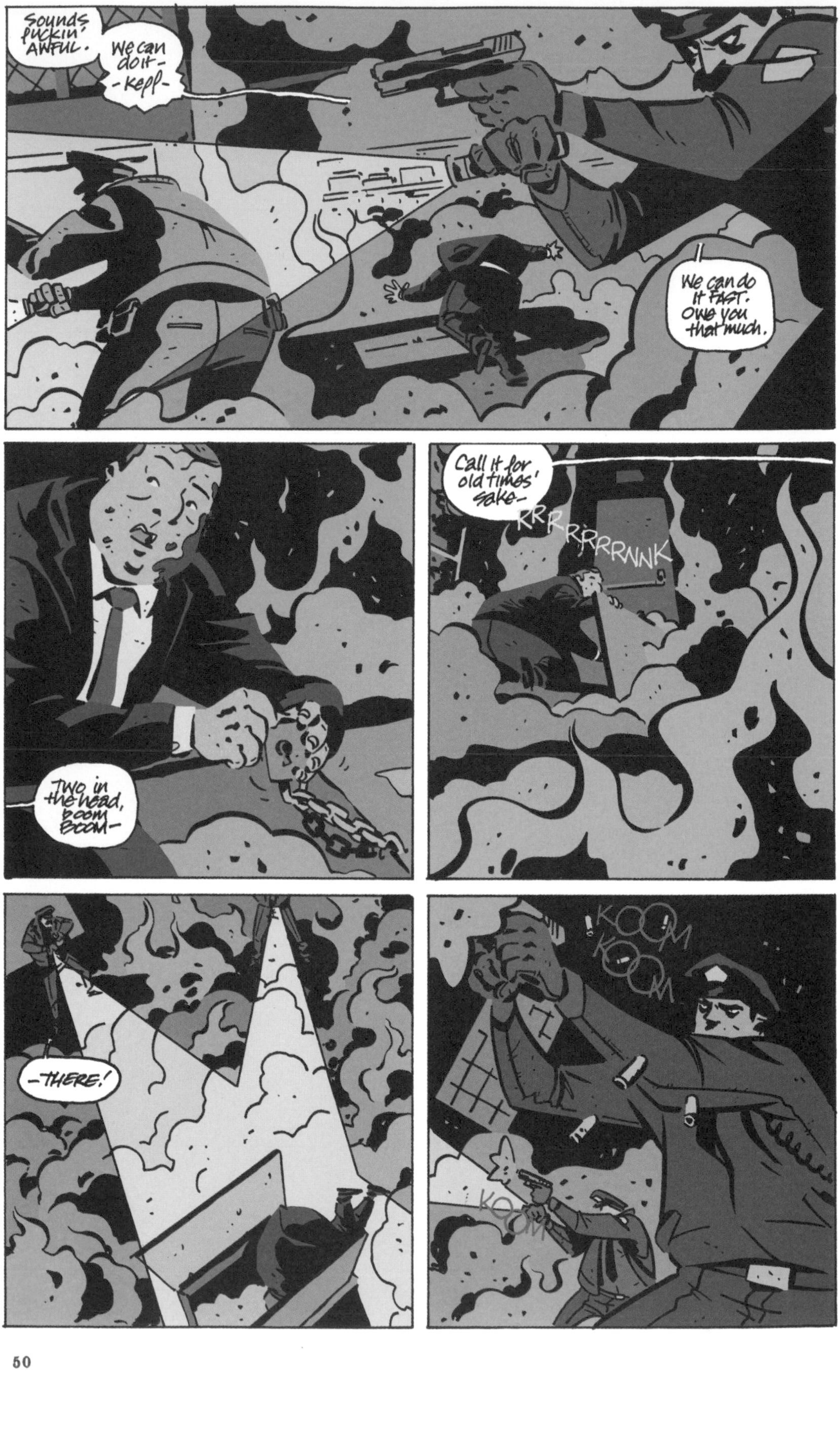
Sounds fuckin' AWFUL.
We can do it— -keff-
We can do it FAST. Owe you that much.
Two in the head, boom Boom—
Call it for old times' sake—
RRRRRRRRNNK
—THERE!
KOOM KOOM
KOOM

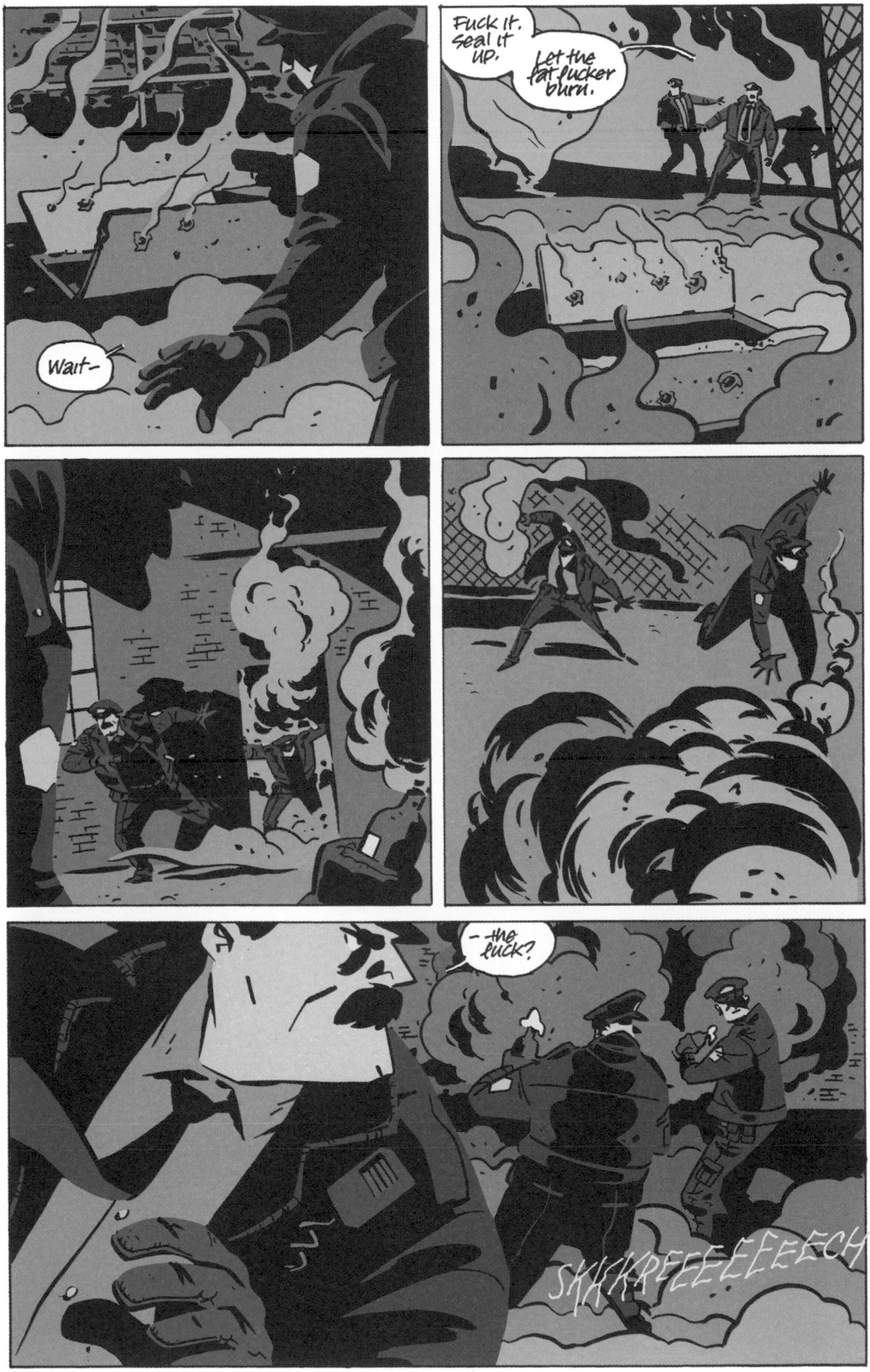
Wait-
Fuck it. Seal it up.
Let the fat fucker burn.
-the fuck?
SKKKREEEEEEEECH

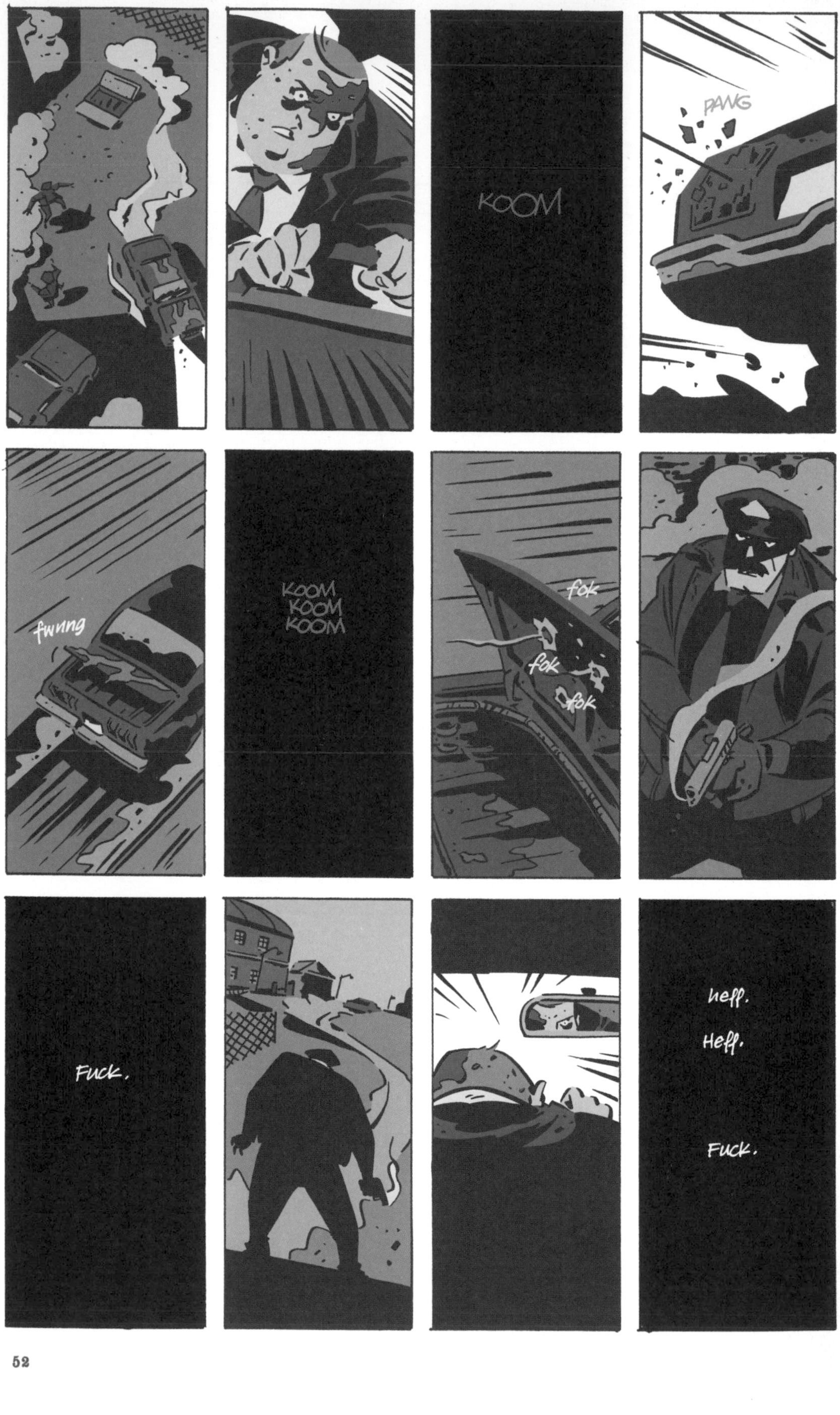
KOOM
PANG
fwung
KOOM
KOOM
KOOM
fok
fok
fok
Fuck.
heff.
Heff.
Fuck.

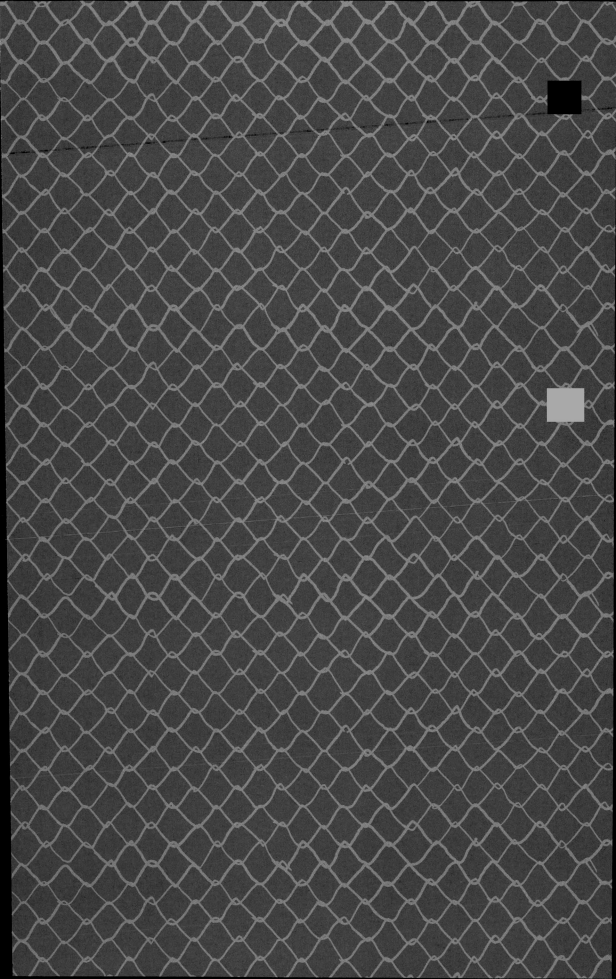

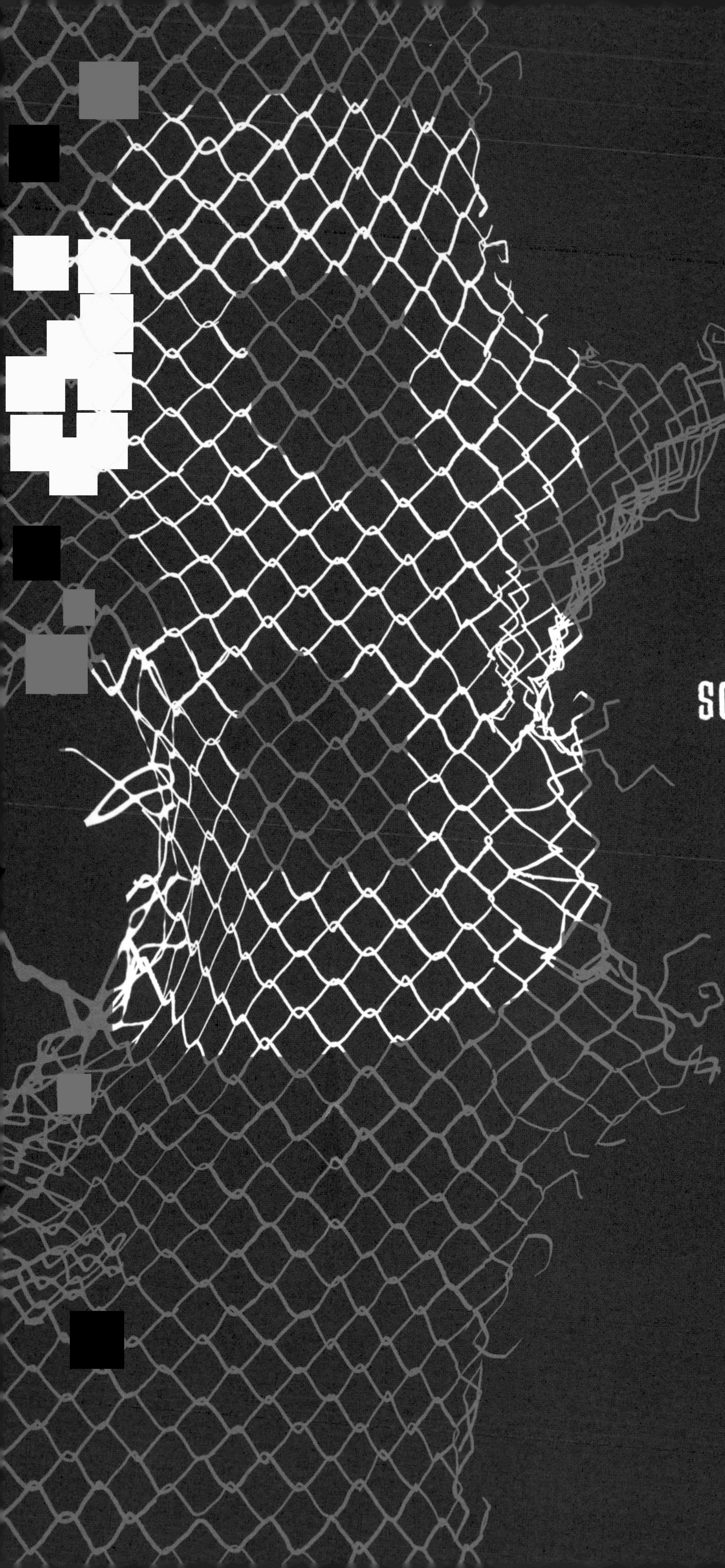

SOME GIRLS

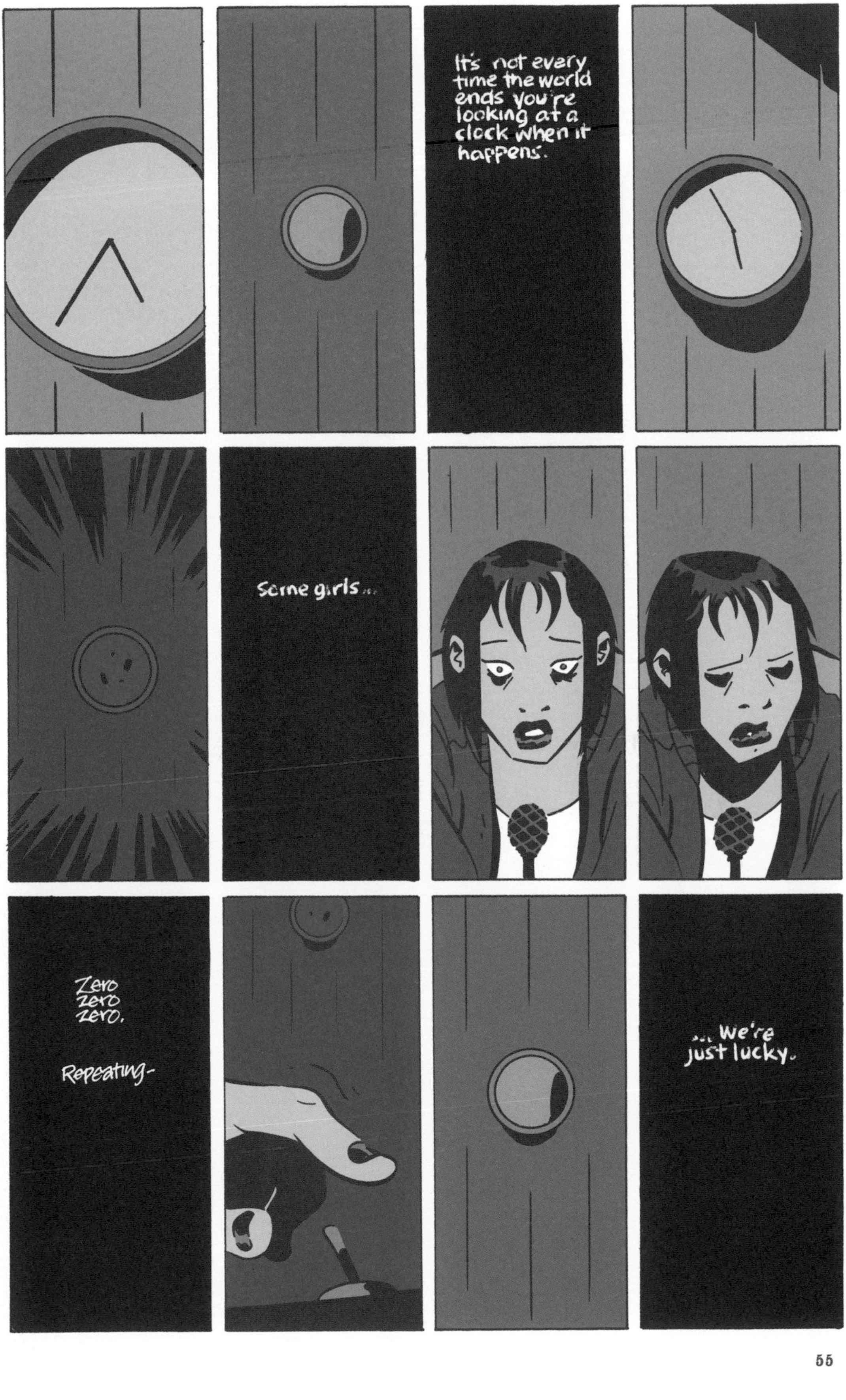
It's not every time the world ends you're looking at a clock when it happens.
Some girls...
Zero zero zero.
Repeating-
...We're just lucky.

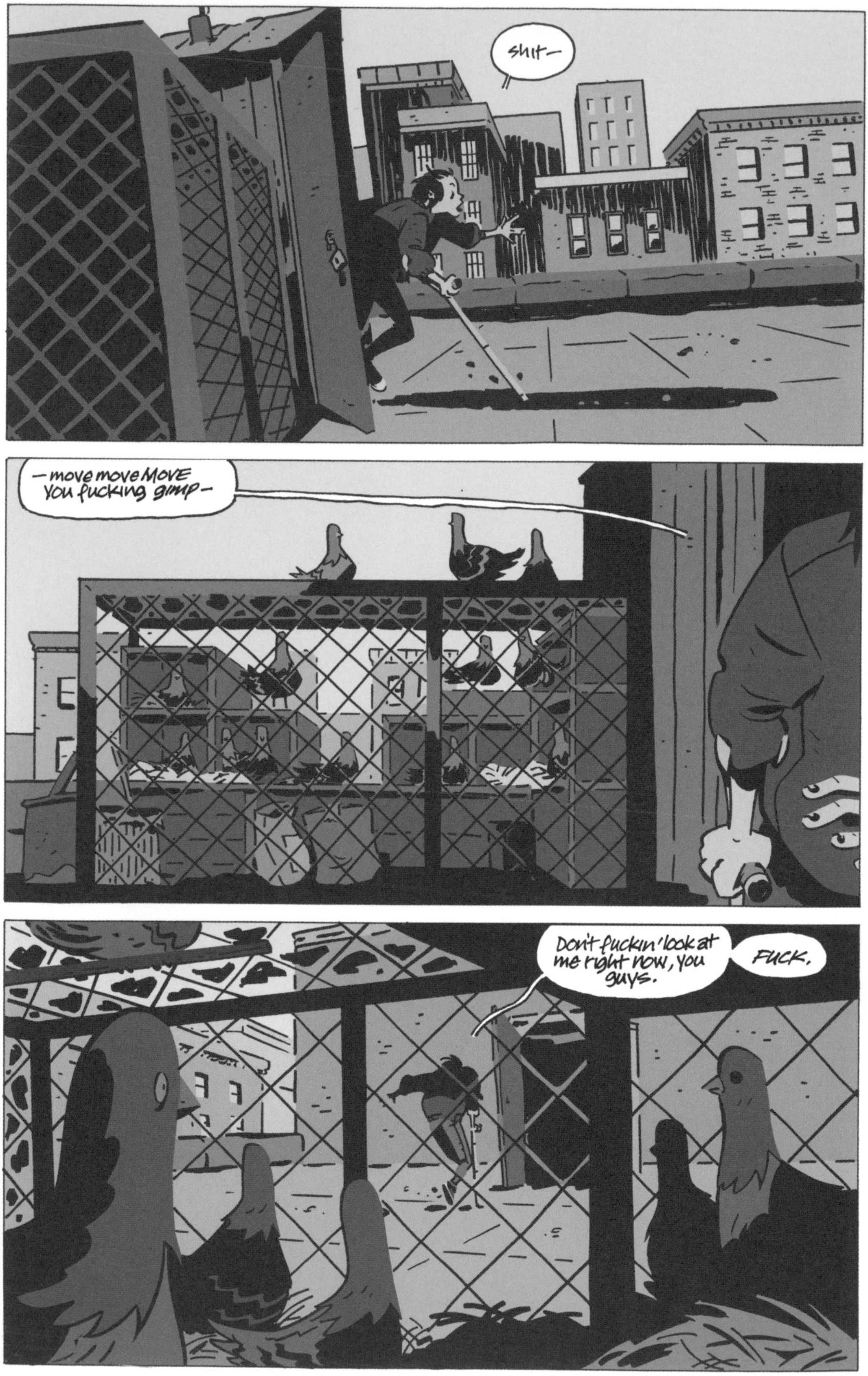
shit—
—move move MOVE you fucking gimp—
Don't fuckin' look at me right now, you guys.
FUCK.

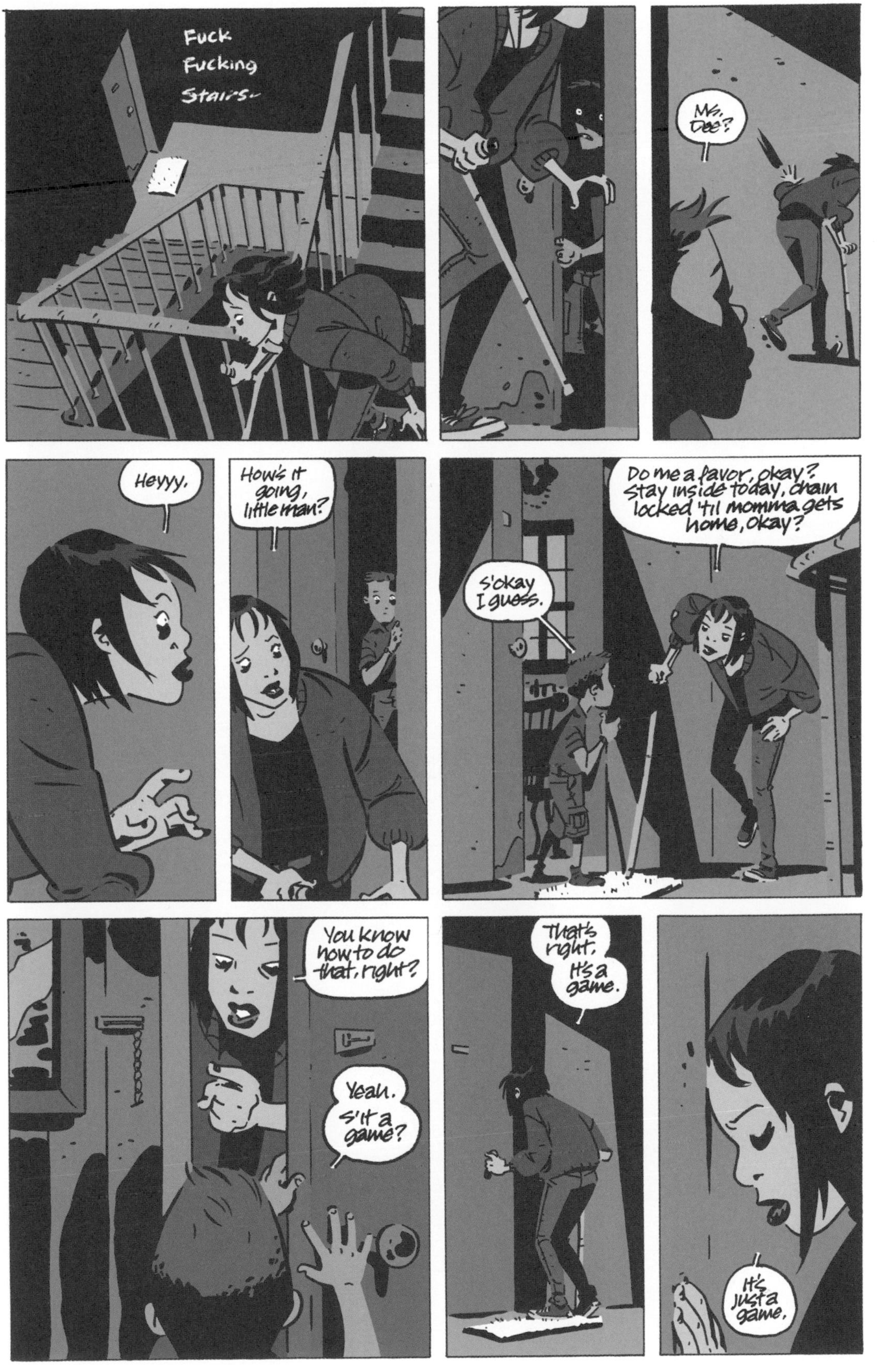
Fuck
Fucking
Stairs-
Ms. Dee?
Heyyy.
How's it going, little man?
Do me a favor, okay? Stay inside today, chain locked 'til momma gets home, okay?
S'okay I guess.
You know how to do that, right?
Yeah. S'it a game?
That's right. It's a game.
It's just a game.

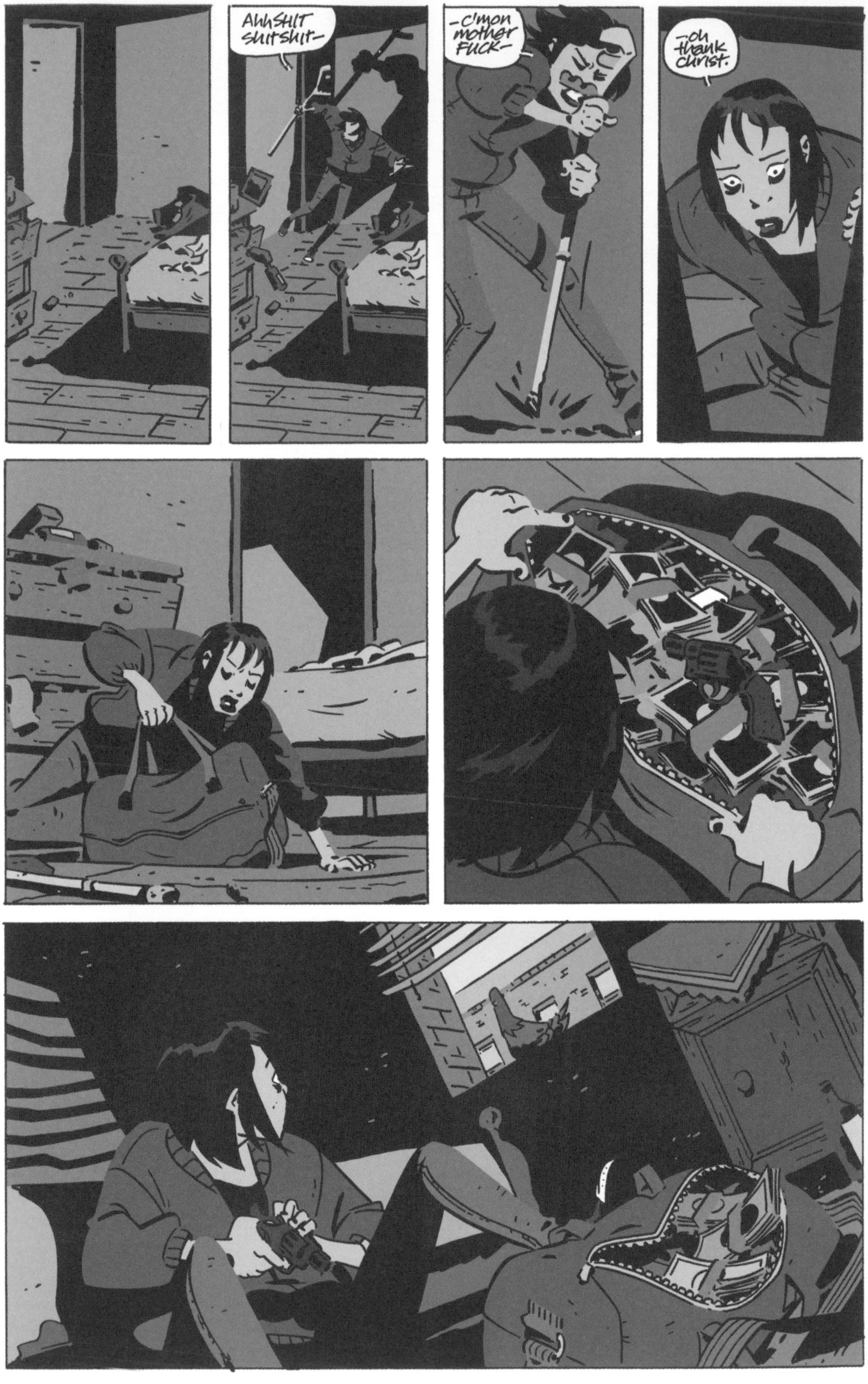
AhhSHIT shitshit-
-c'mon mother FUCK-
-oh thank christ.

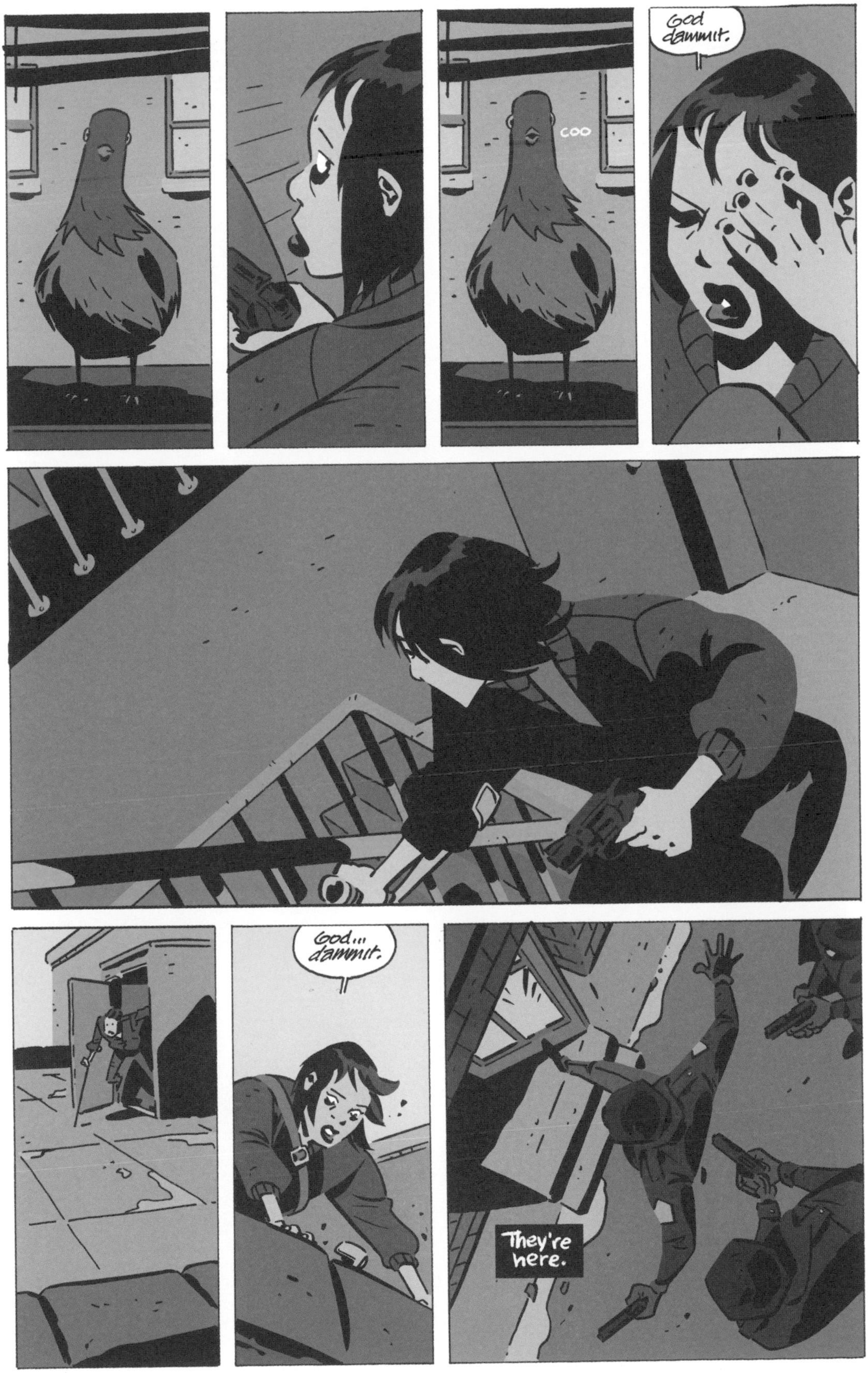
COO
God dammit.
God... dammit.
They're here.

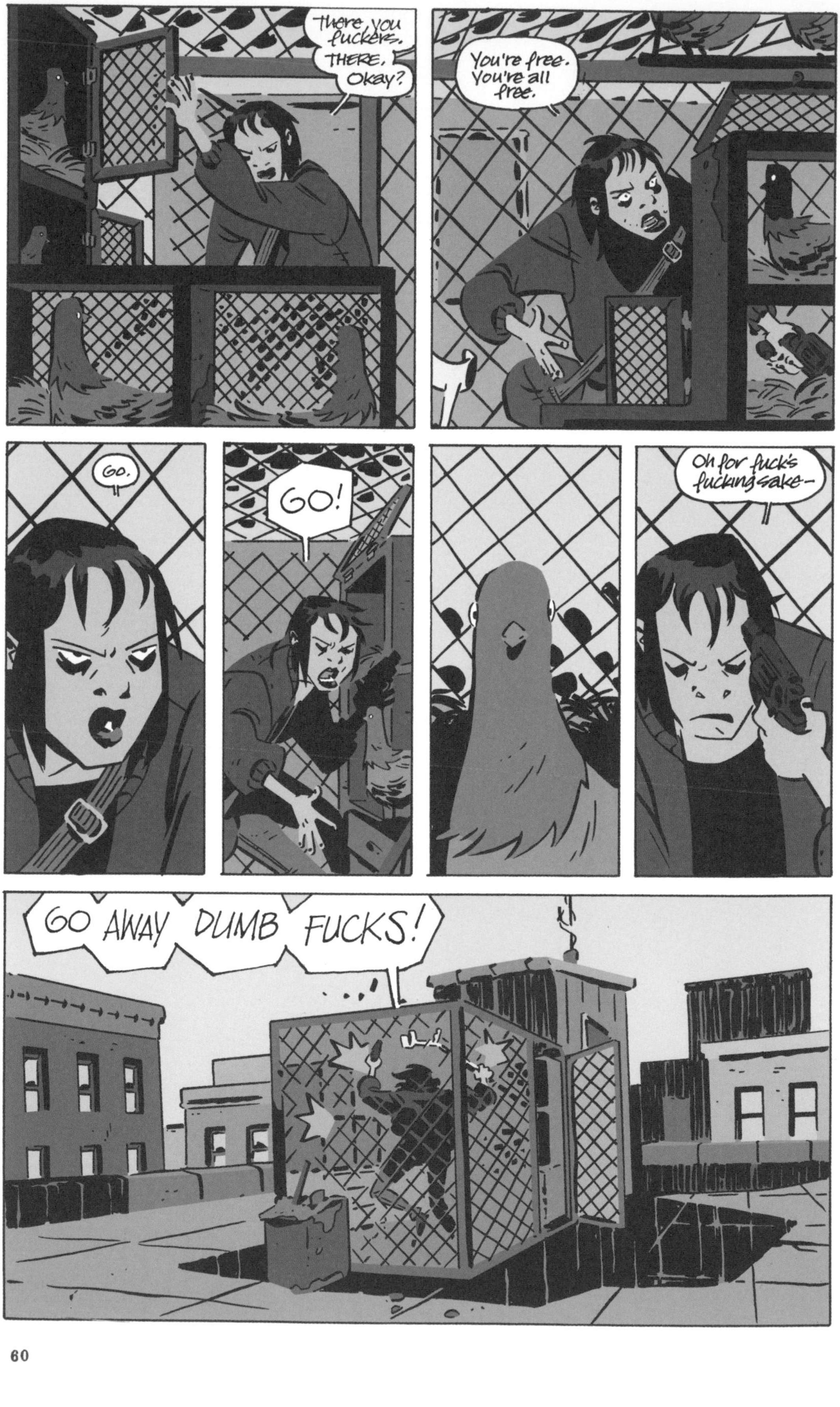
There you fuckers. THERE. Okay?
You're free. You're all free.
Go.
GO!
Oh for fuck's fucking sake-
GO AWAY DUMB FUCKS!

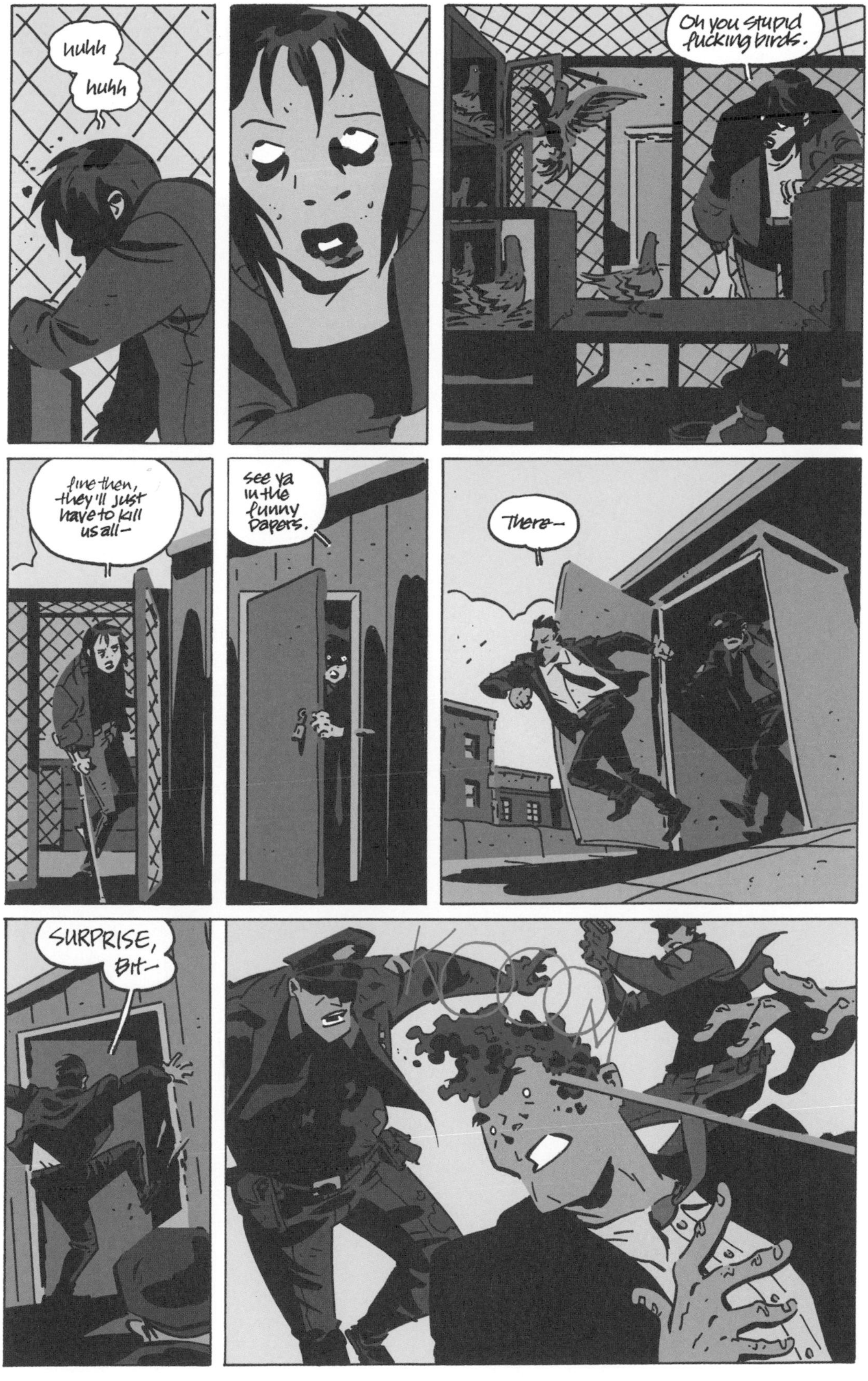
huhh
huhh
Oh you stupid fucking birds.
fine then, they'll just have to kill us all-
see ya in the funny papers.
There-
SURPRISE, Bit-
KOOOM

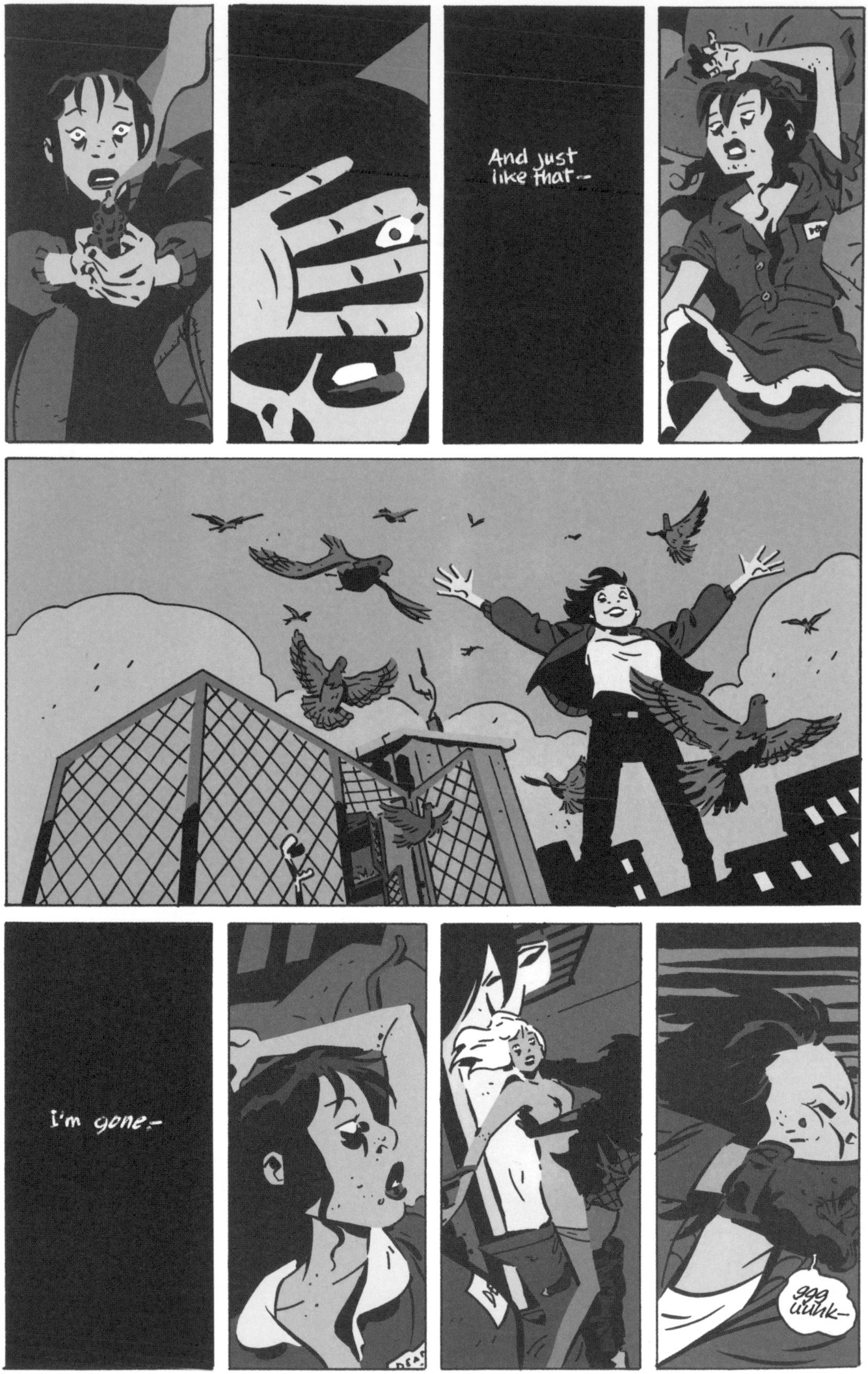
And just like that-
I'm gone-
ggg uunk-

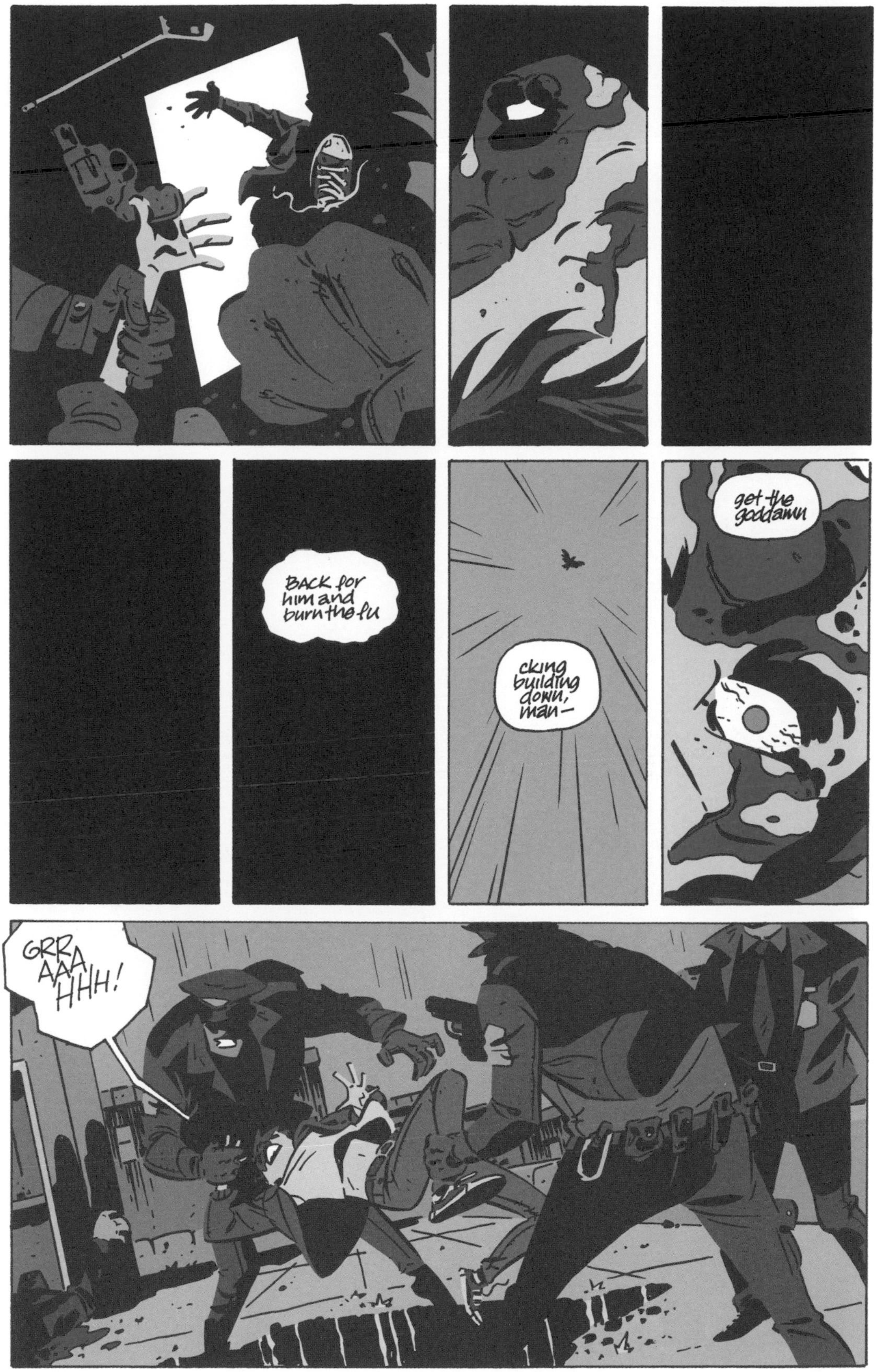
BACK for him and burn the fu
cking building down, man—
get the goddamn
GRRAAAHHH!

JESUS CHRIST—

—like a wild fuckin' animal—

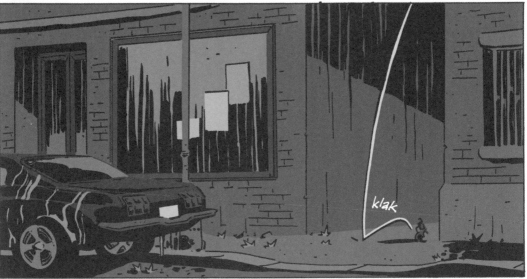

klak

Hit her, fuckin' head, I don't care—

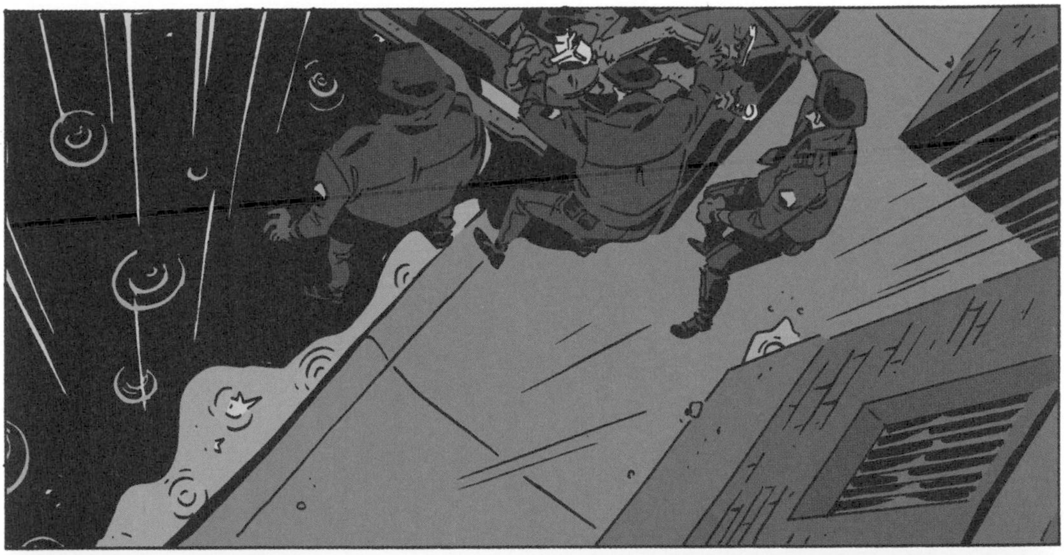

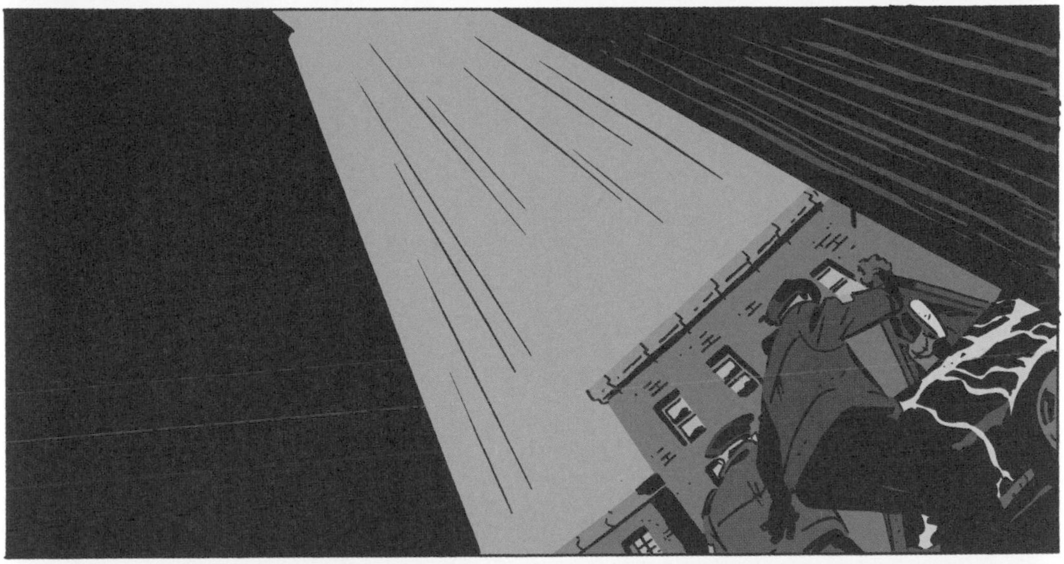

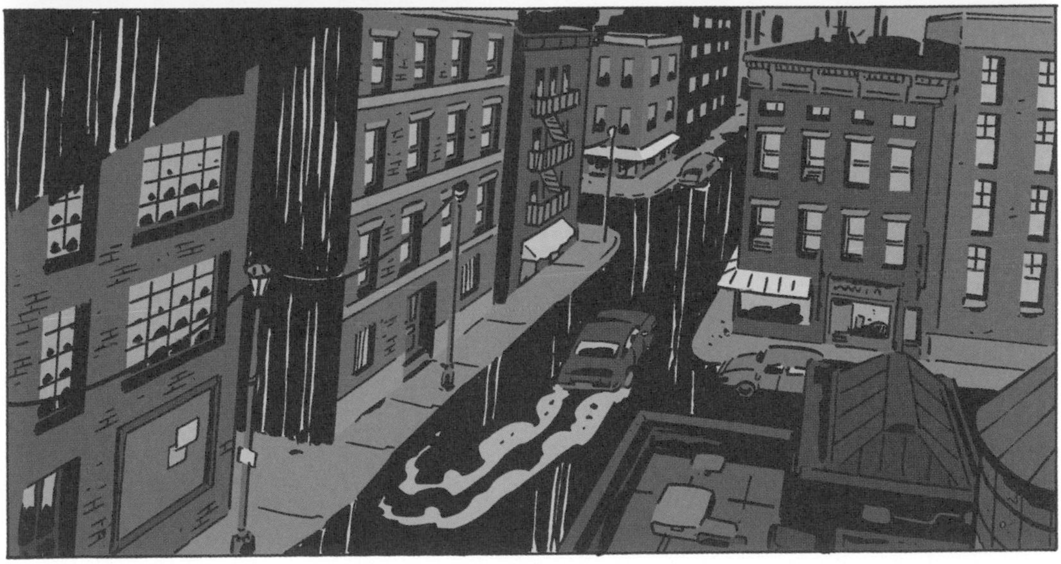

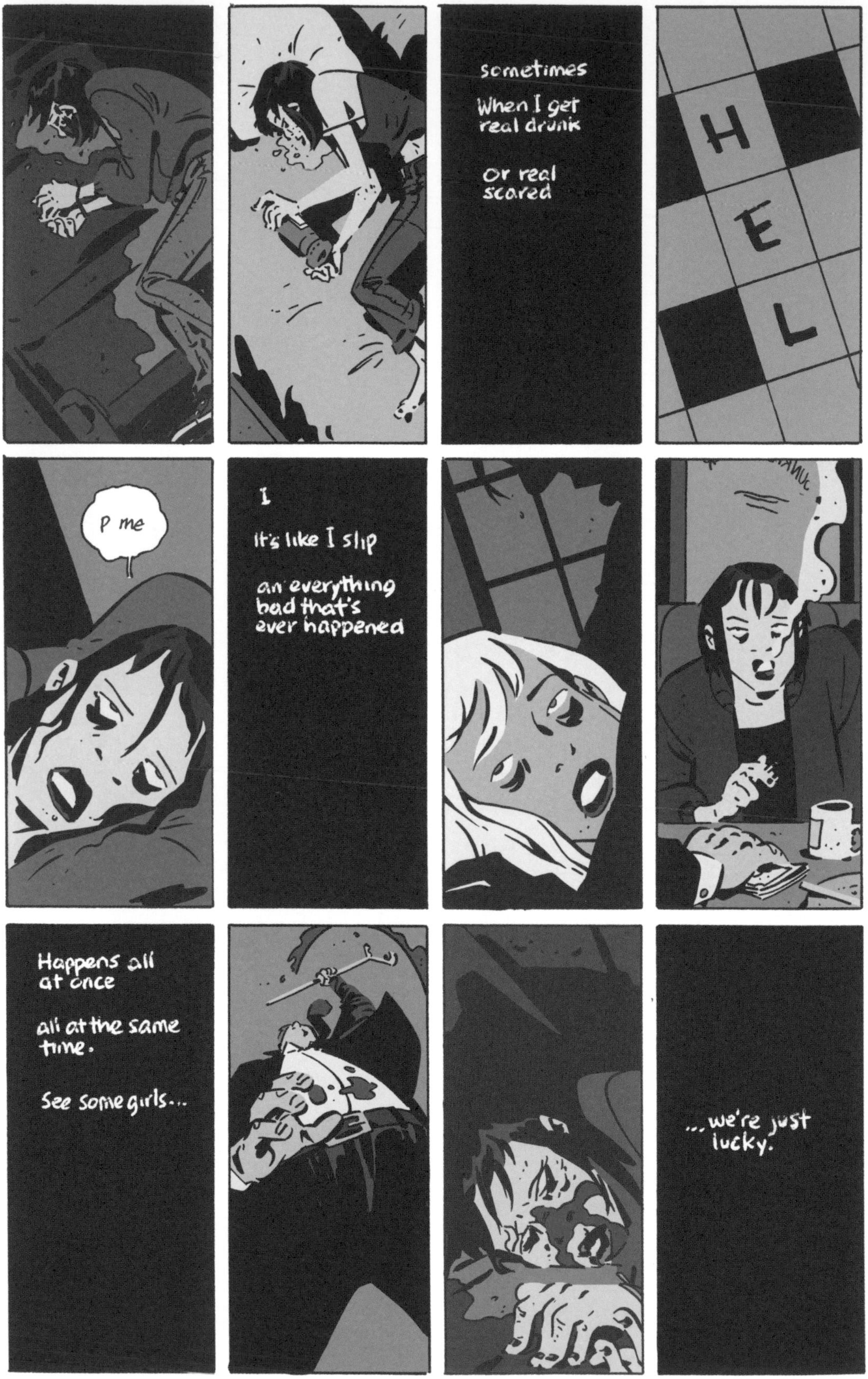
sometimes
When I get real drunk
or real scared
HEL
p me
I
it's like I slip
an everything bad that's ever happened
Happens all at once
all at the same time.
See some girls...
...we're just lucky.

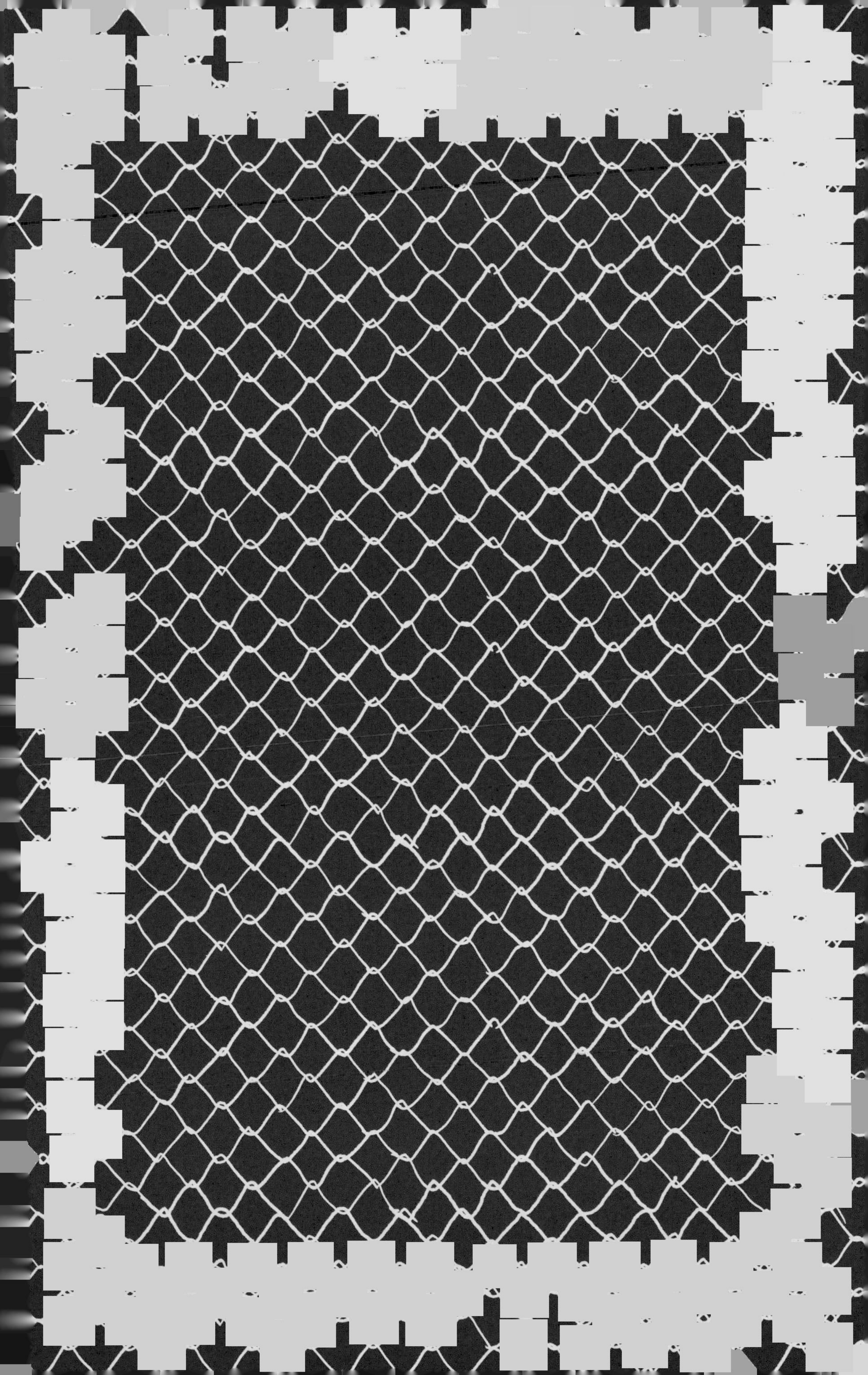

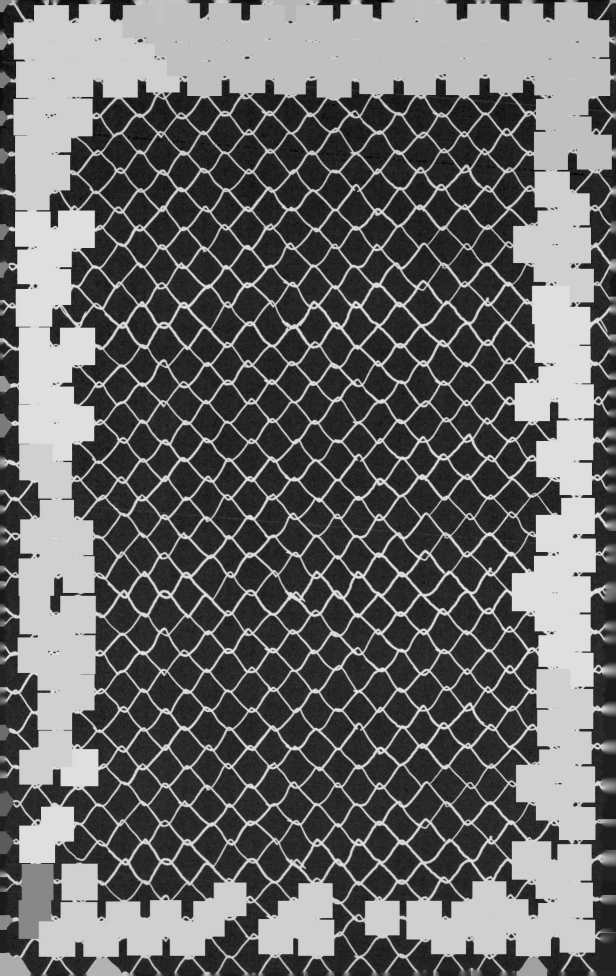

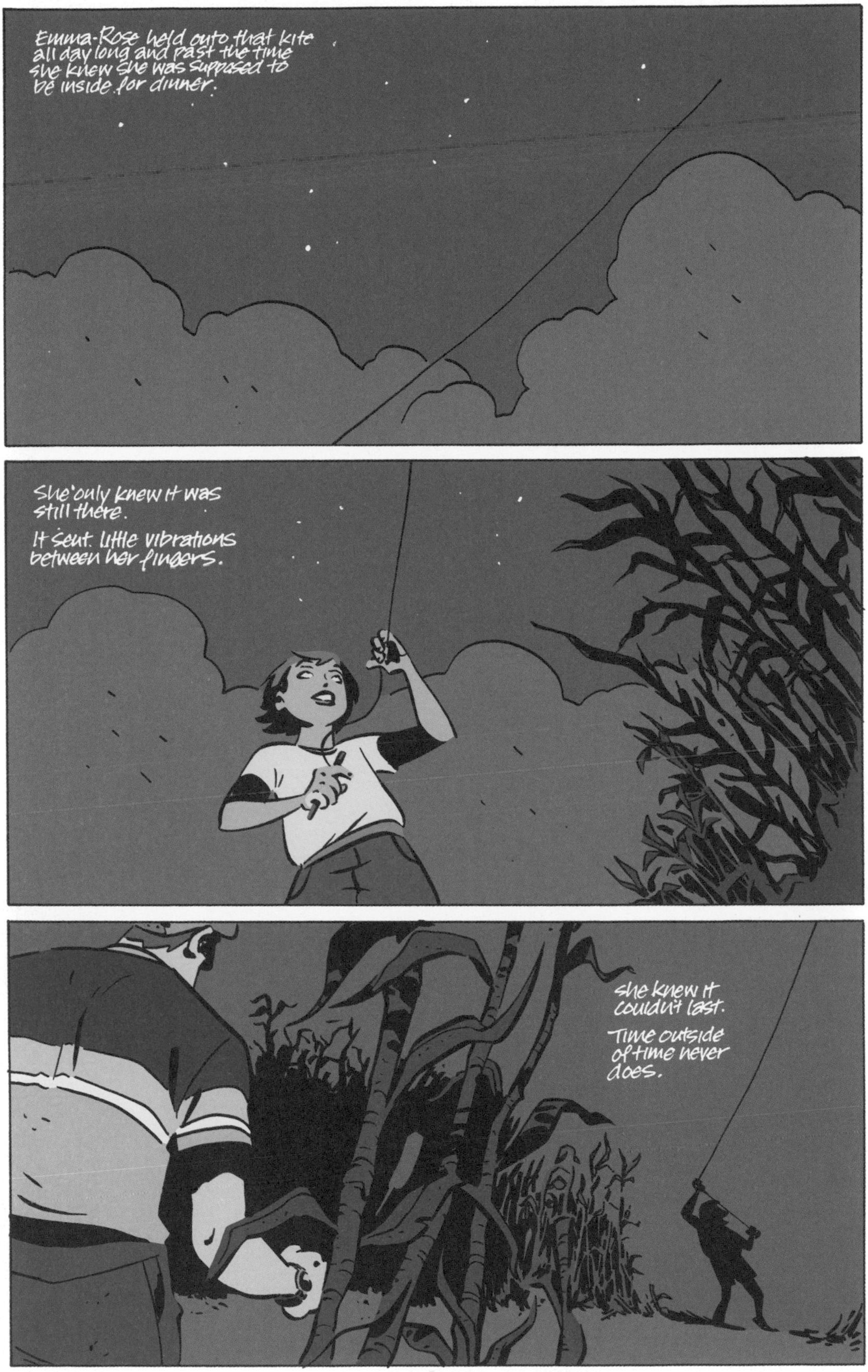
Emma-Rose held onto that kite all day long and past the time she knew she was supposed to be inside for dinner.
She only knew it was still there.
It sent little vibrations between her fingers.
She knew it couldn't last.
Time outside of time never does.

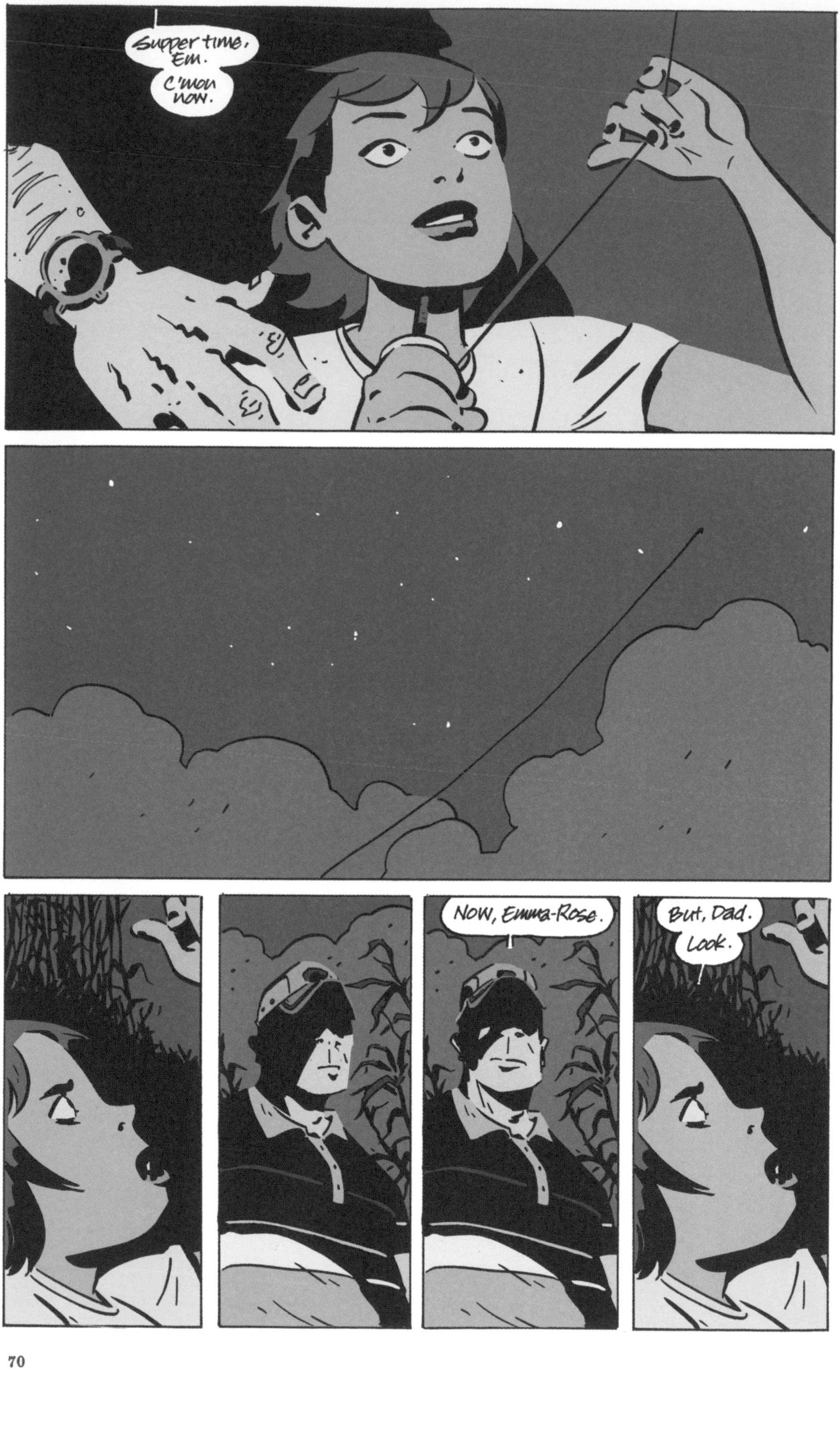
Supper time, Em.
C'mon now.
NOW, Emma-Rose.
But, Dad. Look.

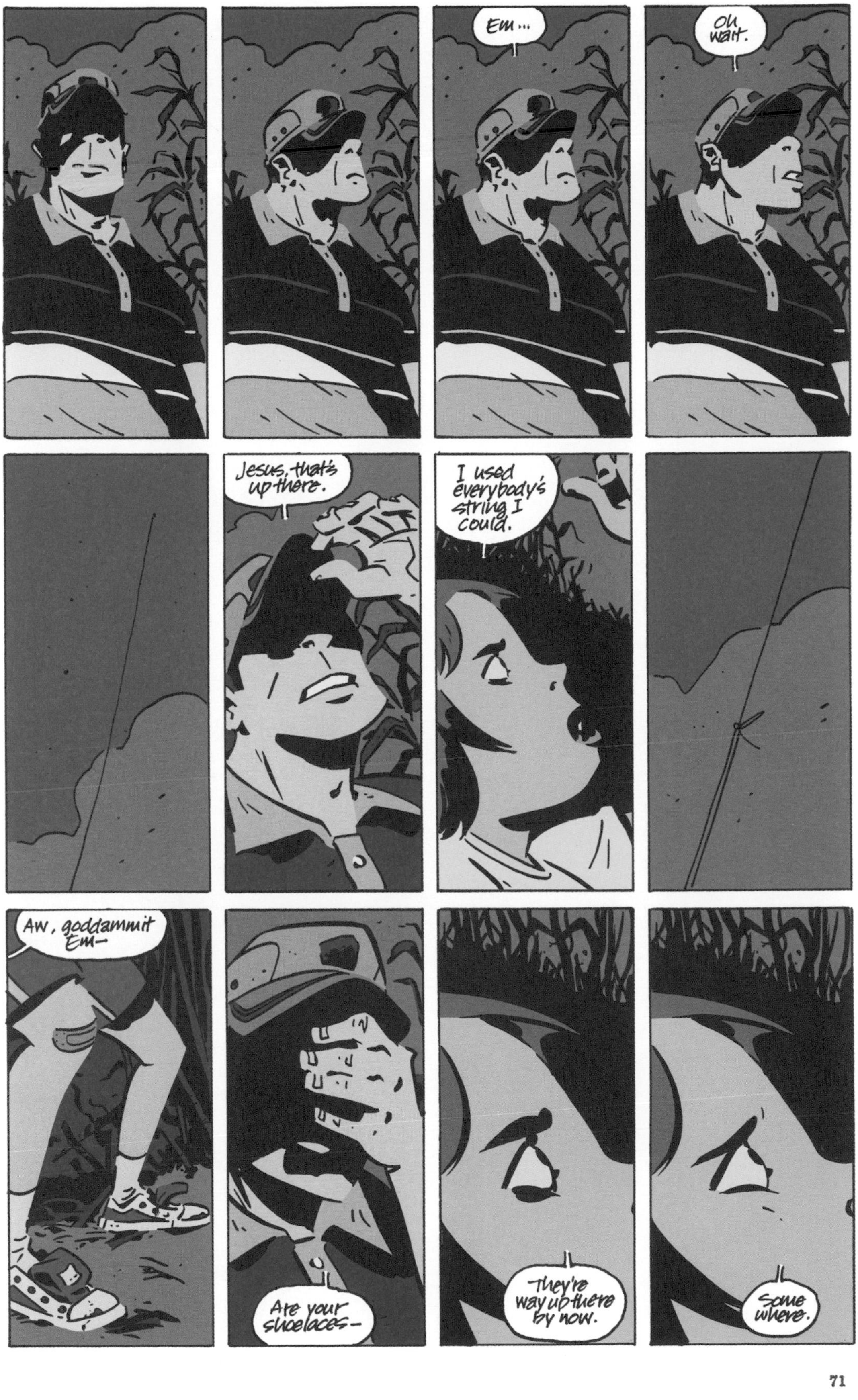
Em...
Oh wait.
Jesus, that's up there.
I used everybody's string I could.
Aw, goddammit Em—
Are your shoelaces—
They're way up there by now.
Some where.

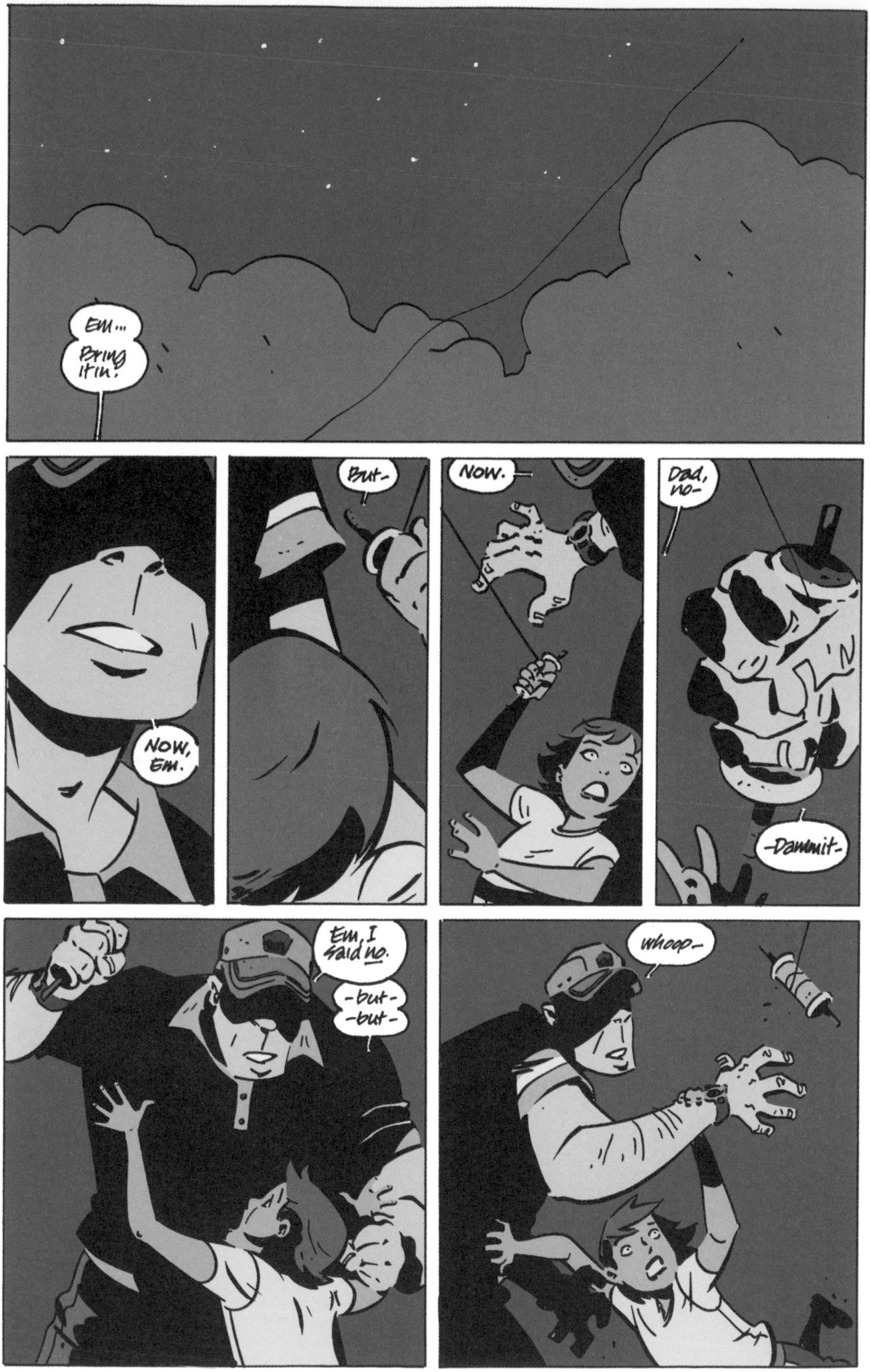
Em... Bring it in.
Now, Em.
But-
Now.
Dad, no-
-Dammit-
Em, I said no.
-but- -but-
whoop-

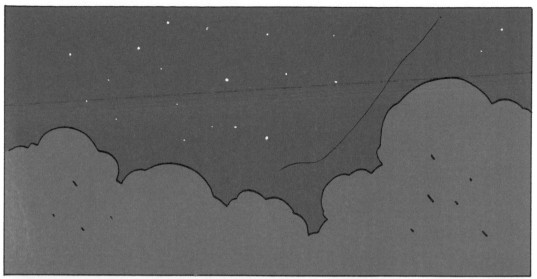

Em...

We're both late for supper, c'mon.

Now.

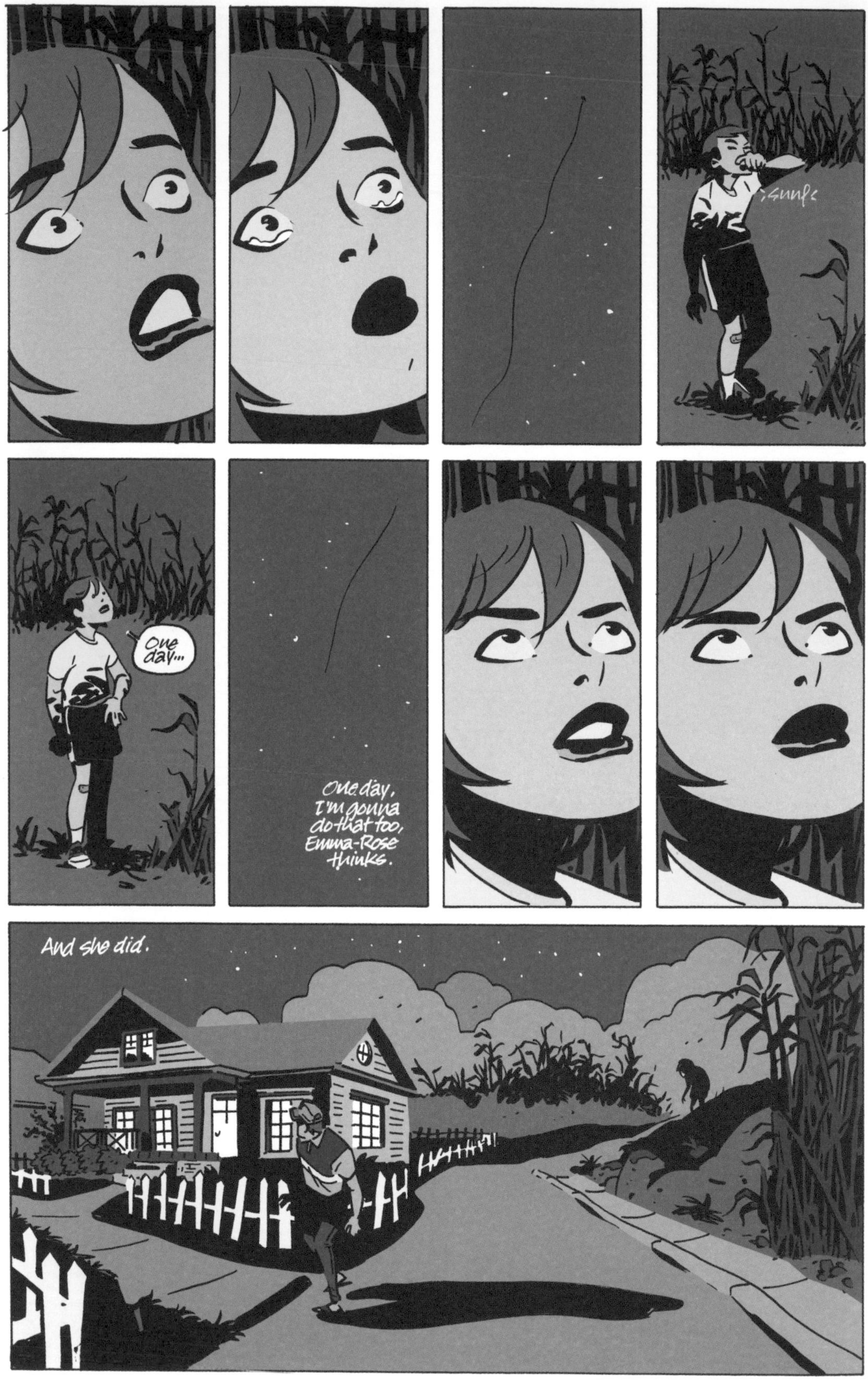

;sunf;
One day...
One day, I'm gonna do that too, Emma-Rose thinks.
And she did.

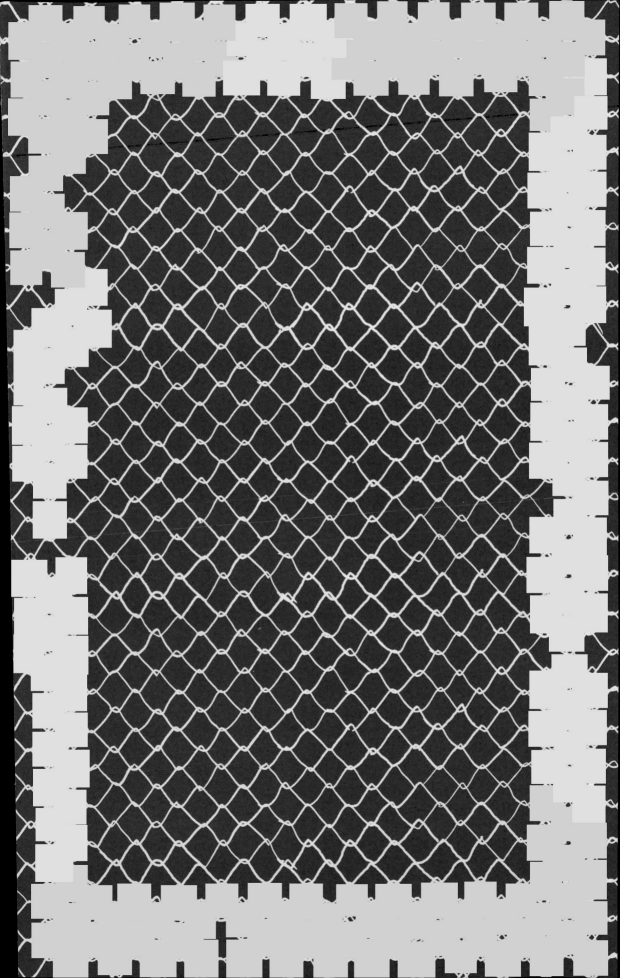

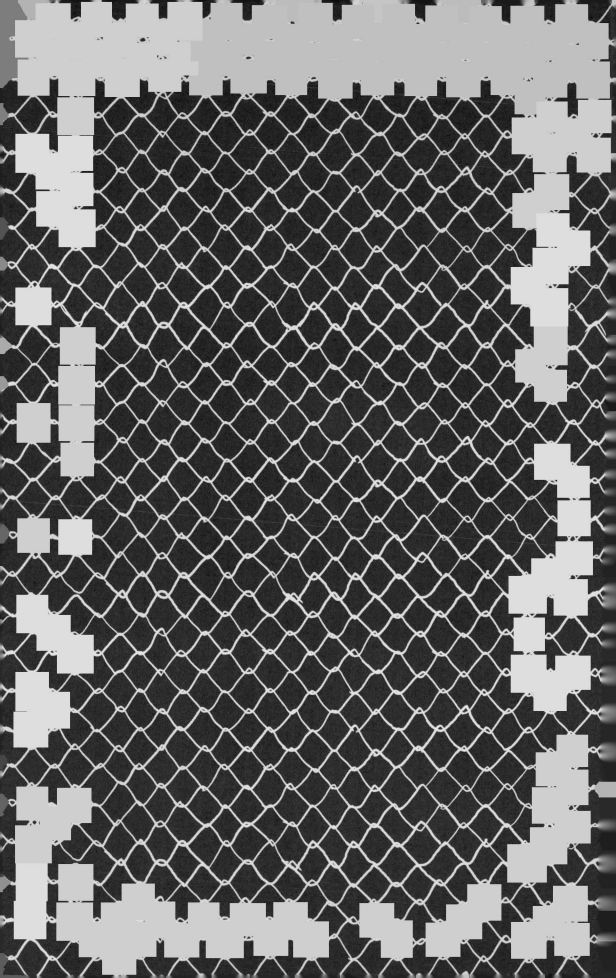

MATT FRACTION
WRITER

ELSA CHARRETIER
ARTIST

MATT HOLLINGSWORTH
COLORIST

KURT ANKENY
LETTERER

RIAN HUGHES
DESIGNER

DEANNA PHELPS
PRODUCTION

TURNER LOBEY
EDITOR

NOVEMBER CREATED BY
MATT FRACTION AND ELSA CHARRETIER

MATT FRACTION writes comic books out in the woods and lives with his wife, writer Kelly Sue DeConnick, his two children, two dogs, a cat, a bearded dragon, and a yard full of coyotes and crows. Surely there's a metaphor there. He's a New York Times bestselling donkus of comics like SEX CRIMINALS (winner of the 2014 Will Eisner Award for Best New Series and named TIME Magazine's Best Comic of 2013), ODY-C, and CASANOVA. Fraction and DeConnick are currently developing television for Legendary TV under their company Milkfed Criminal Masterminds, Inc.

ELSA CHARRETIER is a writer and comic book artist. After debuting on COWL at Image Comics, Elsa co-created THE INFINITE LOOP with writer Pierrick Colinet at IDW. She has since worked at DC Comics (STARFIRE, BOMBSHELLS, HARLEY QUINN), Marvel Comics (THE UNSTOPPABLE WASP), and Random House (WINDHAVEN, written by George R.R. Martin). She has also written THE INFINITE LOOP vol. 2 as well as SUPERFREAKS, and is a regular artist on STAR WARS comic books.

MATT HOLLINGSWORTH has been coloring comics professionally since 1991 and has worked on titles such as PREACHER, WYTCHES, HAWKEYE, DAREDEVIL, HELLBOY, CATWOMAN, THOR, THE FILTH, WOLVERINE, and PUNISHER, among others. He's currently working on BATMAN: CURSE OF THE WHITE KNIGHT for DC Comics as well as SEVEN TO ETERNITY and NOVEMBER for Image Comics. He's won more awards for the beers he's brewed than for the comics he's colored.

KURT ANKENY is an award-winning cartoonist and painter whose work has appeared in Best American Comics, the Society of Illustrators, the Cape Ann Museum, Comics Workbook, Ink Brick, PEN America's Illustrated PEN, and Fantagraphics's NOW anthology. He lives with his wife and son in Salem, Massachusetts.

RIAN HUGHES is a graphic designer, illustrator, comic artist, writer, and typographer who has written and drawn comics for 2000AD and BATMAN: BLACK AND WHITE, and designed logos for James Bond, the X-Men, Superman, Hed Kandi and The Avengers.
His comic strips have been collected in Yesterday's Tomorrows and Tales from Beyond Science, and his burlesque portraits in Soho Dives, Soho Divas. The recent Logo a Gogo collects many of his logo designs for the comic book world and beyond.

IMAGE COMICS, INC.
Robert Kirkman : Chief Operating Officer
Erik Larsen : Chief Financial Officer
Todd McFarlane : President
Marc Silvestri : Chief Executive Officer
Jim Valentino : Vice President
Eric Stephenson : Publisher / Chief Creative Officer
Jeff Boison : Director of Publishing Planning & Book Trade Sales
Chris Ross : Director of Digital Services
Jeff Stang : Director of Direct Market Sales
Kat Salazar : Director of PR & Marketing
Drew Gill : Cover Editor
Heather Doornink : Production Director
Nicole Lapalme : Controller
IMAGECOMICS.COM

NOVEMBER, VOL. 2.
First printing.
May 2020
Published by Image Comics, Inc.
Office of publication : 2701 NW Vaughn St., Suite 780,
Portland, OR 97210.
For international rights,
Contact : foreignlicensing@imagecomics.com.
ISBN : 978-1-5343-1369-9.

For more information on other Milkfed Criminal Masterminds, Inc.
titles, go to www.milkfed.us/books.

NEXT:

THE VOICE ON THE END OF THE PHONE

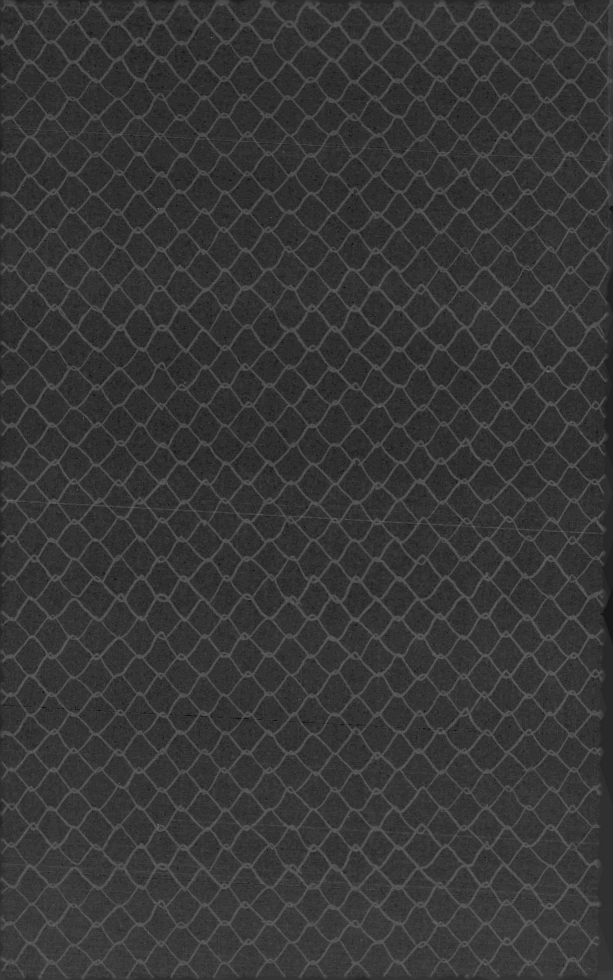